RED HORSE HILL

by the same author

THE BLACK BUCCANEER

DOWN THE BIG RIVER

LONGSHANKS

RED HORSE HILL

AWAY TO SEA

KING OF THE HILLS

LUMBERJACK

THE WILL TO WIN AND OTHER STORIES

WHO RIDES IN THE DARK?

T-MODEL TOMMY

BAT: THE STORY OF A BULL TERRIER

BOY WITH A PACK

CLEAR FOR ACTION!

BLUEBERRY MOUNTAIN

SHADOW IN THE PINES

THE SEA SNAKE

THE LONG TRAINS ROLL

SKIPPY'S FAMILY

JONATHAN GOES WEST

BEHIND THE RANGES

RIVER OF THE WOLVES

CEDAR'S BOY

WHALER 'ROUND THE HORN

BULLDOZER

THE FISH HAWK'S NEST

SPARKPLUG OF THE HORNETS

THE BUCKBOARD STRANGER

GUNS FOR THE SARATOGA

SABRE PILOT

"HERE, I'LL TAKE YE OUT O' THIS"

Red Horse Hill

BY STEPHEN W. MEADER

ILLUSTRATED BY LEE TOWNSEND

HARCOURT, BRACE AND COMPANY

NEW YORK

TO MY FATHER

who will find some old friends
among the characters
in this book

FULL-PAGE ILLUSTRATIONS

RED HORSE HILL

I

THE restless stamping of heavy hoofs woke Bud Martin before it was light. He huddled into a ball beneath the tattered old horse blanket and tried to bury his head in the hay for another snooze. But it was no use. In the next stall old Pompey snorted twice, then, with the noise of an earthquake, scrambled ponderously to his feet. The thick planks shook, for Pompey was the biggest drafter in the Bull's Head Stables—2,500 pounds of bone and brawn—a horse that men turned to look at in the street.

From somewhere down the long line of stalls came a whinny, echoed at once by half a dozen other horses, and Bud heard Pompey blowing in the corners of his crib for stray oats and bits of hay. A stableman came in, humming a tune, and turned on the lights.

"Hey, kid, roll out," he said, and the toe of his boot nudged Bud as he passed. Instantly there was a rumbling growl and out of the hay at the boy's side jumped a three-quarters-grown bull-terrier pup, the hair standing up in a stiff ridge along his dingy white back. Bud grinned and sat up, rubbing the hay-straws out of his eyes.

"Forget it, Tug," he said. "You mean well, but that guy's all right. He's a friend of ours."

The boy got to his feet, took an ancient red sweater, several sizes too large for him, from a peg, and pulled it on over his head. With that his dressing was complete, for he already had on a jersey, overalls and a pair of heavy shoes, considerably the worse for wear. He was a gaunt, rangy youngster, fairly tall but thin almost to the point of emaciation. Lively gray eyes looked out from under the straggling thicket of his brown hair.

"All right, Tug," said he, "let's go." The white dog gave his hand a lick and followed at his heels as he went down the stable floor. At the water-tap, Bud filled a pair of battered pails and began pouring water into the iron troughs clamped to the corner of each manger.

Already from the lower end of the line came a steady *chump—chump*—the rhythmic munching of the horses that had been given their grain. The teamsters began to appear, red-faced fellows in sheep-lined coats, who stamped the snow from their high buckled rubbers and swore at the cold weather. One by one they took curry-combs and brushes from the boxes on the wall and began polishing down the rumpled flanks and legs of their teams.

When Bud had carried water to each of the thirty-six horses on that floor, he took a fork nearly as long as himself and helped Joe, the stableman, pitch hay into the cribs. By that time daylight had arrived. It was seven o'clock, and there was a continual rumble of wagon wheels on the pavement outside.

"Here, boy, go git your breakfast," said the man Bud had been helping. He reached in his pocket and tossed him a dime.

"Thanks," answered the boy. He rummaged in the hay where he had slept and found his cap—a flimsy affair with a flour and feed advertisement printed around its crown. Then he went out, with the lean young terrier trotting at his heels.

It was sharp and cold in the street. A chilly fog hung over the warehouses and tenements of South Boston, and the light snow of the day before still lay packed and dirty in the gutters. Bud started to whistle, then shivered and broke into a run. At the corner was a restaurant and bar where most of the teamsters ate, but Bud knew where he could get more for his money. Down an alley, two blocks farther on, he came to a shabby little lunch-wagon with the name "Dinty's Diner" painted in fancy letters on its side. And in he went, with the dog at his heels.

An active little man in a clean white apron was busy behind the counter. He had curly gray hair and an Irish grin. Two or three early morning customers looked up stolidly at Bud's entrance, then went back to gulping their coffee.

"Mornin' to ye, matey," shouted the cook cheerfully. "What'll yer breakfast be, the day?"

Bud frowned as he studied the bill of fare written on a blackboard over the range. Buying a meal for two out of the funds in hand was a serious matter. "A cup of coffee and doughnuts," he said, finally, "and two cents' worth of something for Tug, here."

"Ja-va!" bellowed Dinty, as if he were repeating an order to a chef in the next block. "Life preservers!" He drew a mug of steaming black coffee with a dexterous twist of the wrist and piled four huge doughnuts on a plate. "Niver mind the two cents," said he. "There's a fine bone here I've been savin' for the pup."

The boy ate slowly, soberly, as if he realized that it might be many hours before food came his way again. Meals didn't happen as regularly as they had when he and his father . . . He stopped eating to swallow mis-

6

erably at the lump in his throat. The memory of the day six weeks before when they brought home Tom Martin's body, crushed by the wheels of his dray, was still very bitter, very vivid in Bud's mind.

He paid for what he had had, slipped the last of the doughnuts in his pocket, and climbed down off the stool. The other breakfasters had departed.

"Here, lad," said Dinty. "Take the bone, an' there's a bit o' ham in the paper for yerself."

"Gee," said the boy, "that's mighty good o' you, Dinty. We'll make out fine with all this." And pulling the collar of his sweater up around his ears, he started back toward the stable.

Tug whined and sniffed at the newspaper parcel. In a corner behind a billboard Bud unwrapped the bone, and for five minutes the hungry young dog gnawed at it ravenously. When at last he had cleaned it of every vestige of meat and marrow he licked his long, powerful jaws and shut them with a contented snap. His master had been dancing a double-shuffle and flinging his arms back and forth to keep warm. Now he set out at a run up the street, and together he and Tug raced for the big Bull's Head sign that hung over the door of the one place they could call home.

The bull terrier got there first, of course, and stood waiting in the entrance for Bud, wagging his white whip of a tail. Just as the boy came up he saw a man's figure loom in the narrow doorway, and then with a sudden yelp of pain Tug was catapulted half way across the sidewalk.

Bud stopped in his tracks, trembling with a cold fury. The man came out, following the terrier belligerently. "Dirty brute, blockin' up my door," he snarled. He wore

a fawn-colored overcoat and a pearl-gray derby hat cocked on the side of his head. Bud knew him. He was Mike Rafferty, owner of the Bull's Head Stables and one of the biggest politicians in the ward. But he had kicked Bud's dog. Deliberately the boy lifted a handful of snow from the gutter and packed it into a hard sphere. Rafferty had taken perhaps ten steps up the street when

8

the snowball left Bud's sharpshooting arm and struck the back of the derby with a solid *sock* that left no doubt of its intention. As the hat flew off, its owner whirled about viciously. But there was no one in sight. Even the dog had disappeared. Rafferty ran back to the alley beyond the stable. It was empty. Muttering ugly words to himself, the ward-leader returned to his battered hat, picked it up, and tried to pound it back into shape. Finally he went into the stable and gave vent to his anger before an audience of teamsters.

It was not until he had taken himself off, still fuming, that Joe, the stableman, strolled to the rear of the floor and called to Bud. The boy was crouching behind a pile of empty feed-sacks, his hand gripped in the piece of old harness-strap that served Tug for a collar.

Joe looked at him for a moment, chewing a straw. "Too bad, kid," he said at length, "but I'm 'fraid you'll hafter make yerself scarce. The last guy 'at knocked Rafferty's lid off was found four days later in the bay with his head stove in. When he went off this time he swore he was goin' to ketch yer an' put yer in Reform School. Rafferty's got pull enough to do it, too; so—"

Bud stood up, looking around him at the dim, familiar place. He squared his shoulders under the red sweater. "Well—guess I'll be goin,' Joe," said he. "Come on, Tug."

"Better go this way," suggested the stableman, point-ing toward the side door that opened into the wagon shed.

9

"Take a couple o' these sacks. They'll help to keep yer warm." He handed Bud a small roll of burlap grain-bags. Then as the boy opened the door he came after him impulsively. "Here," he said in a gruff voice, "here's two bits."

Bud thanked him, put the money in his pocket, and stepped out into the chill half-light of the shed. Most of the wagons were gone, but there were still three or four behind which he could take shelter while he waited to see if the coast was clear. Still holding Tug's collar, he slipped into the shadow of a big dray-wheel, and just at that moment a heavy trampling of hoofs came from the open front of the shed. Peering out, he saw Long Bill Amos leading in his three big Percherons—the matched iron-grays that were the pride of the stable.

Gently the teamster backed his pets into position in front of the dray where Bud was hiding, and let down the double poles between their broad backs. Then he set about fastening the traces and hold-back straps. The boy waited till Amos came around to the side nearest him and was hooking the trace-chain.

"Bill," he whispered, "s-s-st—Bill! Is Rafferty in sight?"

The big teamster stared at him, then went to the horses' heads and looked out. He shook his head. "I don't see him, kid," said he, gathering the reins as he returned. "Here, I'll take ye out o' this." There was an empty sugar barrel lying by the wall, and he swung it up with one hand and stood it on the wagon. "Git in—you an' the dog," he said shortly.

It took but a few seconds for Bud to obey. He found the quarters inside the barrel tight, but by squatting on his heels and holding Tug and the roll of bags in his arms he kept his head below the level of the rim. There was a creak of springs as Long Bill climbed to the driver's seat. Then Bud heard him chirrup to the horses, and with a lurch and a rumble the big wagon swung out into the street.

Some one shouted as they went by the stable door. It sounded like Rafferty's voice— "Hey, where you goin', Amos?" The dray rolled on faster over the cobbles with the big horses at a trot. "B. & M. yards," Long Bill called back. Bud could hear him clucking impatiently to his team. They rounded a corner and the barrel tipped dangerously. For half a dozen blocks the dash continued, while the boy clutched his excited dog and balanced as best he could. Then the clatter of their progress subsided and the grays settled to a walk.

After what seemed a long time Bud ventured to thrust his head above the barrel-top. They were moving along in a stream of heavy traffic through the maze of Boston's downtown streets. He waited till he heard the bell of a shifting-engine and knew they were entering the Boston and Maine freight yards. Then he clambered out of his hiding-place and stretched to get the kinks out of his legs. The dray pulled up alongside the door of a box-car, and

Long Bill swung himself to the ground. As he tucked blankets around the three giant grays he whistled thoughtfully.

"Wal," he said at length, "here ye be, Buddy. An' what next? Ye kin help me load if ye like, but all this stuff goes back within a block o' the stable; so ye'd better stay here in the yards while I'm gone."

For an hour Bud worked with the teamster, heaving sacks of Aroostook potatoes out of the car and piling them on the big wagon. Then he watched his friend drive off and wandered over to the next siding, where a whole trainload of Christmas trees was being un-loaded.

Even now, tied in bundles, with their branches pressed close against their slender trunks, there was a fresh, wild greenness about them and a fragrance of the forest. Clean snow crystals fell from their tips as they were flung on the wagons. Bud looked at them with an odd longing. He had never been in the real woods—never seen firs and spruces growing along mountainsides. But he remembered hearing his mother tell about them. She had lived once where the Christmas trees came from, up in New Hamp-shire.

Just before noon the big gray team came trotting up the yard again with a jingle of harness, Long Bill perched on his lofty driver's seat behind them. He blanketed the horses, filled their nose-bags, and then brought out his own big lunch-box and steaming can of coffee.

"Here, youngster," he called to Bud gruffly. "Come here an' gimme a hand with this."

The boy took the thick sandwich he offered and ate it gratefully, smuggling a piece down to Tug at intervals.

"Bill," he said, "did you ever see trees like them over there—growin'?"

"Sho!" laughed Bill. "I should say so. Down in Maine, where I come from, there wa'n't much else but balsams an' spruces an' pines. Them's New Hampshire trees, there, the yard boss told me."

Bud picked up a spruce tip and fingered its firm, green needles curiously. "Does this line o' railroad run to New Hampshire?" he asked.

"Oh, yes," said Long Bill with a patronizing air. "She runs through New Hampshire on the way to Maine. Now *there's* a state for ye." And he launched on a lengthy description of the wonders of Maine.

Bud heard little of it. He was looking at the twig of spruce and trying to remember the name of the place in New Hampshire where his mother had been born. But it was no use. She had died when he was six, and the years had dimmed his memory of her.

Bill rose and stretched. "Wal," he said, "time to git back to loadin' spuds."

They worked steadily through the chill gray afternoon. It was when they were putting the last sacks on the second load that the lanky teamster straightened up and looked at Bud. Thoughtfully he shot a stream of tobacco-juice over the wheel. "I'll be back for one more load tonight," said he, "an' then I'll take ye home with me. Mebbe we kin find a place fer ye to sleep 'round where I live."

He climbed to the driver's seat, gathered the reins from the backs of the big grays, and drove away.

When he returned an hour later through the gathering dusk he did not see Bud waiting for him. He loaded his dray and then started a search for his young helper, walking up and down the lines of cars, calling, whistling, inquiring of other drivers and freight handlers. Finally he gave up the search and buttoned his coat against the rising north wind. The boy and his dog were gone.

II

IT WAS pitch-dark in the box-car and so cold that Bud could not sleep, however hard he tried. Curled up in a corner under the old grain-bags he had brought from the stable, he held Tug tight in both arms and wondered if they were going to freeze to death.

He had not really planned this journey. After Long Bill Amos had left him in the freight yard he had wandered among the tracks, watching the puffing little engines shunting cars to and fro.

Just as it began to grow dark he saw a big six-wheeler

backing down the yard toward a string of empties on the nearest track. A train going out . . . the night freight to the north. New Hampshire! Right beside him was a B. & M. box-car, its door standing open several inches. Bud looked around, an impulse shaping swiftly in his mind. There was no one in sight. He pulled the car door farther open and swung himself up. With a bound the big young terrier came after him. Bud made a hurried examination of the car and made sure it was empty. Then he pushed the sliding door shut and stood a moment, listening, his heart beating quickly. There was no sound outside except the persistent ding-dong of a locomotive bell and the confused hum of the yard.

The boy took his sacks to the forward end of the car and was trying to arrange them in a sort of bed when a sudden lurch threw him off his feet. A series of clanking jolts followed. The engine was being coupled to the train. Waiting there in the darkness, Bud heard a man go clumping along the top of the car and pause just over his head.

"Hey!" shouted a voice. "What time does Twenty-four go out?"

Some one on the ground answered him. "You've got the right o' way. Twenty-four's bein' held till you're clear."

The brakeman went on to the next car, and in a moment the train got under way with a jerk. A slow progress across innumerable frogs and switches followed,

16

but at last the freight settled down to its methodical, jogging gait. The monotonous click of the rails was a lulling sound, and Bud was very tired. Again and again he started to doze off, only to be bumped back to wakefulness by the hard boards on which he lay. Tug slept fitfully in his arms, shivering sometimes and uttering little moans that were half snores. Then the cold came, biting through the coarse burlap and the ancient sweater and making Bud's teeth chatter.

A wind from the north was blowing. It rattled the loose-hung doors of the car and whined fiercely around the chinks and corners. Bud squirmed his shoulders and hugged the body of the dog against him. Miserably he remembered the warm hay and the pungent, horsy smell of the Bull's Head Stable.

Once or twice the train stopped to pick up cars at small-town sidings, but in spite of the cold Bud stayed where he was. He had started for New Hampshire, and he was no quitter. As the hours dragged by he had time to do a lot of thinking. What would he do when he got there? As far as he could recall he had never been a dozen miles from Boston in his life. All he knew about the country was got from the few books he had read and the stories his mother had told him. Surely he would have been wiser to stay in the city, where at least he knew the streets and had a friend or two. And yet, since his father's death Bud had come to hate the town.

"No," he muttered doggedly, "I'll go there an' see, anyway."

For half a dozen years Bud had had to take care of himself. He and his father had lived in two furnished rooms, but Tom Martin's working-hours were long, and his boy saw little of him except at night.

Bud had gone to school some of the time, depending on whether he liked the teacher and whether the truant officer could catch him. For the most part he wandered around the docks and the stables. When he needed food he ran errands, did odd jobs, or sold papers. He had never joined any of the neighborhood gangs because of a certain stubborn independence that was part of his character. He had fought it out with more than one gang leader, and afterward they had been glad to let him alone.

For all the torturing cold the boy must have dropped asleep at last, for when an unusually hard jolt shook the car he sat up suddenly, rubbing his eyes, and found that a faint gray light was coming in around the door. The train had stopped, and he could hear men's voices and an occasional jingle of sleigh-bells outside. Tug was standing with his nose at a crack, sniffing the frosty morning air. As quietly as possible Bud opened the door a few inches and looked out. The car was on a siding flanked by lofty piles of snow. Down the track a hundred yards was a frame station building with a black and gold sign. "Riverdale," read Bud. Where had he heard that name before? It had something to do with horses—race horses.

Then he remembered. He had seen posters advertising Riverdale Fair, with pictures of wide-nostriled trotters tearing down the stretch. Riverdale, New Hampshire! He had really reached his goal.

The boy put his hand into his pocket and drew forth the battered relic of his lunch-wagon doughnut and the piece of ham that Dinty had given him. "Here, pup," said he, "this is our breakfast. Eat slow and make the most of it."

The advice was wasted on Tug. At a single snap he gobbled his half of the rations and sat with hopeful eyes while his master finished the rest.

Bud wiped the crumbs from his mouth with the back of a dirty hand, pulled the old sweater tight around him, and peered up and down the track. There were railroad men at work a dozen cars away, but none seemed to be looking. The boy jumped down into the snow and started in the direction of the station. At that moment he heard a yell behind him. He and Tug must have been seen leaving the car. Like a flash he scrambled under the couplings and emerged on the other side of the train. There were more box-cars before him, and a freight shed, its platform piled with a jumble of boxes. Twisting and doubling like a pair of jack rabbits, the boy and his dog ran on until both cars and shed were between them and their pursuers. A narrow alley opened ahead, and they sped down it. At the end was a larger street, bustling with morning activity.

As soon as Bud was sure he was no longer being chased he stopped by the curb and gaped at the strange sight that met his eyes. There was not a wheeled vehicle passing. Instead he saw work-horses pulling heavy wagon bodies mounted on bob-sleds. Sleek trotters went by, hitched to shining sleighs, and rough-haired farm nags in the shafts of homely two-seated boxes on runners. The snow, heaped in tall drifts along the gutters, was packed firm and smooth in the roadway, and all these conveyances moved swiftly, to the pleasant accompaniment of many-toned bells.

There were none of the tall, dingy buildings he was used to seeing. Instead the street was lined on both sides with solid frame houses and low, comfortable-looking business blocks of sunny red brick. A granite bank stood on the corner, and beyond it opened a roomy square with a fountain and watering-troughs in the middle.

Across the square, as he watched, there came a huge automobile, tall and massive like most of the motor cars of that day. Its radiator and gas lamps gleamed with bright brasswork. A uniformed chauffeur in goggles bent above the wheel and guided its ponderous advance. A constant squawking of the horn hustled the sleighs out of the way to left and right. The car came chugging down the street and stopped impressively in front of a three-story office building almost opposite where Bud stood.

A large, pompous-looking man in a black fur coat climbed out of the tonneau, said a word or two to the

20

driver, and entered the building. In the car sat a boy of twelve or fourteen with a plump, pale face. He stared across at the youngster on the sidewalk, eyeing his ragged red sweater superciliously. Bud flushed. "Come on, Tug," he muttered, and started to walk away. He had taken half a dozen steps when he realized that the dog was not trotting at his side. Looking back he saw him standing like a gray-white statue, the hairs lifted in a stiff ridge along his back. And in that instant a big Airedale jumped out of the parked car and came bounding over the snow.

There were no preliminaries. Like a black-and-tan thunderbolt the newcomer charged down on Tug. The next second the two dogs were mixed in a flurry of whirling bodies and the air was full of a breathless, incessant snarling. Bud ran back, shouting Tug's name at the top of his voice, but he could not make himself heard above the din of the battle. Twice he tried to reach in and seize the strap on his dog's neck. The second time a flashing snap of the Airedale's teeth ripped his sweater from elbow to cuff. A crowd had begun to collect. "Look out there, kid," a man cried, and pulled Bud away.

The chauffeur and the sallow-faced boy came hurrying across the street, the latter jumping around excitedly and screaming something about "tramps" and "dirty curs."

"Go get him, Archie! Kill him!" he yelled, encouraging his dog.

But Archie was no longer having the best of it. He was taller and many pounds heavier than Tug, but the bull terrier could take care of himself. Young as he was, his whole life from puppyhood had been a succession of battles. And his blood was fighting blood. His ancestors for a century back had been warriors, trained for the pit. Instinctively now he dodged and whirled, always keeping his feet, always waiting his chance. It came soon. The Airedale lunged too far, and in a split second Tug's mighty jaws clamped shut on his throat. This way and that the rough-haired dog hurled his body in a frenzied effort to pull away, but the white terrier had his grip. The Airedale's snarling was now only a succession of hoarse gurgles.

"Break 'em loose!" some one cried. "He'll kill him as sure as guns!" Two men seized Tug by the hind legs and pulled vainly. A teamster ran up with a heavy whip and lashed the white dog till some of the crowd interposed.

"Get the police! Get a fire-hose!" people were shouting.

Bud fought to get through the press of onlookers once more. He could hear the strangled gasps of the Airedale and catch glimpses of Tug's white body braced rigidly against the desperate thrashing of his adversary. Finally the boy succeeded in squeezing through. At once he dropped to his knees by Tug's side and gripped the dog's strap collar.

"Tug," he said, "let go! Let go, Tug! Let go, I tell you." The young terrier's eyes had been closed to the merest slits, blind to everything but the grim pleasure of holding on. Now they opened and his forehead wrinkled back with a questioning look at the insistent command in his master's voice.

"Let go, Tug!" Bud repeated, and again, "let go!" his tone growing sharp with fear, for the Airedale was staggering on limp legs. For a moment more the boy's will and the white terrier's killer instinct struggled. Then the boy won. Stiffly the terrible jaws opened, and with heaving sides the rough-haired dog slumped down in the snow.

At that moment, through the close-packed crowd a burly figure in blue came shouldering.

"Here, what's the meanin' o' this?" roared a big voice. And Bud, who had an inbred terror of policemen, made the mistake of trying to duck out between the bystanders, pulling his dog after him. Half a dozen hands laid hold of him, and squirm as he would he could not slip out of their grip.

"They was fightin', chief," said one of the men importantly, dragging Bud toward the officer. "This kid's dog purty nigh killed Sam Felton's 'fore we got 'em apart."

Laughter from the crowd greeted this account of the affair, and for a moment the constable seemed undecided what to do. Then the big man in the black fur coat came hurrying across the street.

"Pa," screamed the pasty-faced youth, dancing about in the snow, "look what they did to Archie!"

His parent stooped above the Airedale, now beginning to recover but still somewhat the worse for his encounter, then strode over to Bud and the white terrier. A glance at the strap around Tug's neck, and he turned angrily toward the policeman.

"Here, chief," said he, "this is what comes of letting stray curs hang around the town. We've got a dog-license law. Where's this brute's collar and tag?"

The constable frowned at Bud. "You hear that?" he growled. "Where's his collar and license number?"

Bud shook his head miserably. "That's the only collar he's got," he answered.

"Look here," said the officer, coming a step closer, "where do you live, anyway?"

Desperately the boy looked around for a way of escape, but the crowd had formed a tight ring about him. He stood silent, pulling at a raveled yarn in the sleeve of his old sweater.

"Speak up, boy," the constable rumbled. "Ain't you got a home?"

"No," said Bud, "I guess I haven't got any home at all."

The pompous, fur-coated man turned to the officer with a gesture of impatience. "He's a common vagrant, chief," said he. "Ought to be made to move on at once, or else be put in the lock-up. As for the dog, I'd advise you to shoot him before he does any more damage. That Airedale of mine is a valuable animal."

24

It was at this juncture, while the policeman was still hesitating, that a short, thick-set figure in a mackinaw pushed through the on-lookers.

"Wait a minute, Ben," the newcomer said mildly. "You ain't aimin' to arrest a boy this size. As for the fight, it was Felton's dog started it. I seen the whole business. I'll take keer that they don't git in any more trouble. Jest leave 'em to me."

Without more ado he reached out a big mitten for Bud's hand and made a path for the boy and the dog through the crowd.

III

BUD had walked the best part of a block before he had a view of his new friend's face. Then the man looked down at him with a grin. "Come pretty close to landin' in the calaboose that time," said he. He looked fifty or thereabouts, a stockily built man with a weather-tanned face and a close-clipped gray mustache. Shrewd, good-humored wrinkles played around his eyes and mouth.

He had on a brown fur cap that came down over his ears, and his feet were incased in knee-high felt boots and buckled rubbers.

They stopped beside a hitching-post where a fat sorrel mare drowsed between the shafts of an old sleigh.

"Now, let's see," said the man, pushing up his cap

and scratching his head. "First of all what's yer name, buddy?"

"That's it," the boy replied. "They call me Bud. My right name's Hartley Martin."

"Hm, Hartley, eh?" said the other. "That's my wife's maiden name. Some o' your relatives live 'round here?"

"My mother came from New Hampshire," Bud answered. "Hartley was her name, too."

"And you ain't got any home, you say?"

"Not any more. I used to live in Boston until I came away yesterday. All my folks are dead."

The man nodded understandingly. "So you're just sort o' looking 'round," said he. "Well, now, if you've got other plans you don't have to do this, but Aunt Sarah an' me would be real pleased to put you up fer a few days, up at the farm. That'll give you a chance to git your bearin's an' decide what next."

Bud looked at his feet. "I haven't got any money," he said.

"Sho'!" laughed the other. "I wasn't figgerin' ye had. Guess a boy as big as you kin help enough around the place to earn his keep. Ever been on a farm?"

"No," replied the boy doubtfully. "But I'm good with horses. I can drive a three-horse truck through Boylston Street traffic without touchin' a wheel."

"Gosh!" exclaimed the farmer, as he took the blanket off the mare. "Hear that, Betsy? This boy an' you ought to make good friends."

He pulled out a massive silver watch. "Time we was hikin' out fer home if we want any dinner," he said. "Move some o' them bundles off the seat, Bud, an' pull that buff'ler robe up around you. The pup can set in the box, behind there."

With a pleasant jingle of sleigh-bells they jogged across the square and up a long street lined with elm trees toward the outskirts of the town. Almost as soon as they were clear of the houses they began to climb. Bud looked back and saw Riverdale spread like a toy village in the level stretch of valley by the river. They swung off the highway after a mile or two and set out on a narrow country road that wound upward past scattered farmhouses. Great billowing hills rose along the horizon, the nearer ones a frosty gray, and those more distant fading in mysterious blue.

Bud stared at them, big-eyed. "Gee!" was all he could say.

The farmer pointed off to the left with his whip. "That long ridge is Hogback Mountain," said he, "over in Danford township. And this round, high one with the snowy top, straight ahead, is Blue Job. That's where we live, up on the southwest shoulder. If you look real hard you can see a red barn showin' up against the snow."

Bud shaded his eyes and squinted across the miles of gleaming white. This was a new experience for him. He felt a queer lump in his throat—partly homesickness for the dingy canyons of the city he knew—partly joy in the great sweep of the snow-covered hills. "Yeah," said he, "I can see it plain. And a lot o' woods, too." He wondered if there were any Christmas trees up there.

In spite of the sunshine it was cold out here in the open where the wind blew. Bud shivered and pulled the tattered buffalo robe tighter around his chest. The driver of the sleigh looked down at him. "That ain't a very warm outfit, son," said he. "We'll have to fix you up with some old duds o' mine. Say—you look kind o' peaked. What was the last meal o' real victuals you set down to?"

Bud grinned a twisted grin, for he had been trying to forget the gnawing pangs inside him. "I got some coffee an' doughnuts yesterday mornin'," he answered, "and a fellow gave me a sandwich at noon."

"Jumpin' Jehosaphats!" cried the farmer and laid the whip across the plump flank of old Betsy. "Why didn't you tell me, Bud? I'd have filled you up in the White Front Lunch! Well, anyhow, we'll be home in half an hour."

They moved faster after that, for the mare knew she was nearing home and trotted with head up and ears pricked forward.

Through a stretch of woods the road led and then swung upward between brush-grown stone walls. A hilly pasture, rough with junipers and outcropping ledges, rose on the right.

"Here we be," said the driver of the sleigh. "We're

climbin' Red Horse Hill this minute. Soon as we git over this rise we'll be right in the yard."

Above the snowy crest of the hill Bud saw a weather-vane shaped like a trotting horse, silhouetted clear against the blue sky. Below it, as they climbed, there slowly appeared the cupola and roof of the barn and the tops of bare maple trees. Then he saw a neat white house with green shutters, connected with the barn by a long inclosed shed. On the R. F. D. box by the fence the name "John Mason" was stenciled.

The mare reached the top of the slope and swung eagerly into the snowy yard.

In front of the granite doorstep Mr. Mason pulled her to a stop. "Easy, Betsy," he said. "I'll git you fed in a minute, but this boy here's a heap sight hungrier 'n you be."

He jumped out of the sleigh and took an armful of groceries. "Come on, Bud," said he; "let's see what Aunt Sarah's got fer dinner."

For the first time Bud felt shy. Climbing out from under the buffalo robe, he looked down at his ragged sweater and incredibly dirty overalls. "Gee," said he, "I—" But his words were interrupted by the appearance in the open door of a plump gray-haired little woman with rosy cheeks and shining spectacles. She smiled, looking from her husband to Bud and back again.

"Mother," said Mr. Mason, with a twinkle in his eye, "here's a young relation o' yours I picked up down to Riverdale. His name's Hartley Martin. Bud, this is Aunt Sarah."

There was no doubt about the welcome in Mrs. Mason's smile. "Come right in," said she. "You must be cold from that long ride. Yes, the dog, too. He can stay by the stove an' git thawed out. The cat's gone to the barn after mice, so there won't be any trouble from her."

She led the boy through an entry-way into the immaculate kitchen. "Guess you'll want to wash 'fore dinner. There's the wash-basin and the towel," she directed, and bustled away to set another place at the table.

Bud filled the basin from the iron pump at one end of the sink and set about scrubbing the collected grime of days from his hands and face. One grew careless about such matters at the Bull's Head Stables. As he dried his dripping arms, a savory odor came to him from the steaming pots and pans that bubbled on the range. In all his hungry life no food had ever smelled so good. Tug sniffed it, too. He crouched by the stove, his mouth wet with anticipation and his tail drumming the linoleum in quivers of eagerness.

There was a stamping in the shed beyond the kitchen, and Mr. Mason came in, pulling off his mittens and mackinaw.

"Wal, Bud," he grinned, "think you'll be able to take a little nourishment?"

He had his turn at the wash-basin, and as he finished,

his wife appeared with the news that dinner was ready.

The red-and-white checked table cloth awed Bud a little. It had been years since he had sat before such splendor. A napkin, too! He bowed his head awkwardly during the brief grace and struggled to remember some of the table manners his mother had taught him as a little boy. Even after a plate of steaming corned beef and cabbage and mashed potatoes was set in front of him he watched his hostess to see how she held her fork. But after the first mouthful he forgot his embarrassment and ate with a zeal that made the Masons smile at each other across the table. When his second big helping was finished there was pumpkin pie for dessert, and milk— all he wanted to drink. "There," said Mr. Mason at last, "that's better. Now we'll see about givin' that white scrapper o' yours somethin' to eat besides Airedale fur."

When the dishes were done Mrs. Mason sat down in the big rocker by the dining-room window with her sewing-basket and an old suit of her husband's. "My land!" she said, eyeing Bud's attire. "It's a wonder you didn't freeze solid in that freight car last night. The clothes I'm goin' to fix for you won't be stylish, but at least they'll keep out some o' the wind."

Bud, inclined to silence at first, was soon won over by her kindly interest. Gradually he told her all his story, winding up with his sudden decision to find New Hampshire, where his mother had once lived.

"I wonder, now," mused Mrs. Mason. "You say she was a Hartley. What was her Christian name?"

"Jane," said Bud.

"It don't seem hardly possible," the farmer's wife continued, "but do you suppose she could have been the Jennie Hartley that used to go to school in Riverdale just before I was married? She was Silas Hartley's daughter. Their farm was on the old Danford Road, up on the mountain above Caterwaul River—"

"That's it!" cried Bud excitedly. "Caterwaul River! She told me how she caught a fish there once. An' it was named Caterwaul because it kept mewing like a cat when it ran down over the stones."

"Well, sakes alive!" said Mrs. Mason. "Then you *are* a relation, sure enough. John, do you hear that? This boy's Jennie Hartley's child. Let's see, now; her father, Silas Hartley, was a cousin o' my father's. What would that make us? Well, anyhow, Bud, you've found your folks. I wouldn't be surprised if we were the closest kin you've got 'round here. Cousin Silas didn't have any other children, an' after he died the house stood empty for years. Last summer it burned down—struck by lightnin'. It's a lonesome place up there in the woods. I don't know who owns the farm now."

"That settles it," said the farmer, with a twinkle in his eye. "After this you're to call us by our proper names —Aunt Sarah an' Uncle John. An' unless you've got other plans you'd better count on settlin' down right here —till cold weather's over anyhow."

By the time the winter dusk began to fall Bud's made-over suit was ready. To a critical observer it might have looked a bit odd and old-fashioned in cut, but it was honest wool, thicker and warmer than any clothes the boy had ever owned. He could hardly wait to put it on.

"You're goin' to sleep in the west attic room," said Mrs. Mason. "I'll take you up there now, an' you can change."

Bud was conducted up a steep dark flight of stairs to a cozy chamber under the peak of the roof. There was a square window, level with the floor, and a solid-looking old cherry four-poster with a bright quilt of patchwork across its foot. It was cold, of course, for there was no stove in the room, and the door at the foot of the stairs was kept shut.

Left to himself, Bud stood on a braided rug and stripped. He pulled on the old suit of winter underwear and wool socks that the farmer's wife had found for him, then donned the trousers and jacket and his own worn shoes.

"You look a sight more respectable," said Mrs. Mason when the boy appeared in the dining-room once more. "We'll have to do somethin' to make you fill 'em out more, though. They fit as graceful as a sack on a bean-pole now. Here, give me the old ones. We'll wash 'em and see if there's anything left."

34

Mr. Mason looked in from the kitchen. "Come on, Bud," said he, "let's go 'tend to the stock."

He led the way out through the shed, carrying a lantern that threw weird bobbing shadows along the walls. Beyond, a door opened into a second, larger shed where a top-buggy and a two-seated "Concord wagon" stood and sets of harness hung on long wooden pegs. Then came the barn itself.

Bud saw a long, dim, dusty floor, littered with hay-straws. Huge mows of hay reached upward into the gloom on one side. Along the other were stalls, with feed-windows facing the open space in the middle of the barn. A warm, pleasant smell came to Bud's nose, and he could hear bodies moving—the creak of stanchions and the rustle of straw. Tug, who had been at his heels, trotted here and there, sniffing at things with interest. Mr. Mason opened the door into the "tie-up."

"Here they are, son," said he, holding up the lantern over a row of brown backs. "Grade Jerseys—nine of 'em—the best butter-makers in Riverdale Township. An' here's Old Betsy's box-stall over in the lean-to. You might take a fork an' put some clean straw in there for her bed while I git ready to milk."

The farmer hung the lantern on a hook, bedded the cows, took his three-legged stool and a shining pail, and set to work. Bud watched open-mouthed, for he had never seen a cow milked before. The musical drum of the jets of milk fascinated him.

"Gee," he said at last, as Mr. Mason's strong hands deftly stripped the last drops into the foaming pail, "do you suppose I could ever learn to do that?"

"Ho!" chuckled the farmer. "I should say so. When I was your size I was milkin' five every night an' mornin'. Soon as ol' Daisy starts to dry up, in a week or two, I'll let you practice on her."

"What do you do with the milk?" asked Bud.

"Put it through the separator," said Mr. Mason. "The cream we make into butter, an' I sell it to my reg'lar customers down in Riverdale. The pigs an' calves get the skim-milk."

He showed Bud how to carry the full pails into the shed and bring back clean empty ones. In an amazingly short time he had milked all the cows in the row. Then water was carried to the stock, and a night ration of hay, and they returned to the house. The farmer placed the buckets of milk in a line beside the brightly gleaming cream separator in the kitchen. Slowly he started turning the crank of the machine, timing the revolutions by his big silver watch. When it had picked up speed to a vibrant hum he made a signal to his wife, who strained the first pail in at the top. A thin stream of golden cream and a thick one of snowy milk began pouring from the nozzles into empty pails set to receive them.

When the separating was finished they fed the pigs, quartered at the back of the barn, and then supper was ready.

Bud still had a ravenous appetite, but he almost fell asleep over his third sugared doughnut.

"If you don't mind," he said, "I guess I'll go to bed now. I didn't sleep so very much last night in that box-car."

Mrs. Mason gave him a nightshirt and a candle, and looking into his tired face, leaned forward suddenly and kissed his cheek.

"There," she said, "now you run along up. I'll fix a good bed for the dog in the shed."

Bud got red, mumbled a good night, and climbed the stairs. He hadn't been kissed for six years except by Tug. Wearily he slipped off his clothes and crawled into bed.

"Golly," he muttered, "guess I'm a lucky kid . . ." and in three seconds he was sound asleep.

IV

WITH the first gray light of morning Bud sat up in bed, rubbing his eyes. For just a second he could not recognize the little clean room with its sloping ceilings. Then a grin spread over his face as he remembered. He was out of bed in an instant and jumped into his clothes like a fireman. Cheerful sounds of activity from below and the chilly air of his chamber lent speed to his dressing. Stumbling down the stairs, he opened the door into the dining-room with a breathless "Good morning!"

Mrs. Mason was setting the table for breakfast. "Well, for heaven's sakes!" she cried. "Up already? I expected to have to call you."

"I came down to help milk again," said the boy. "Has he gone out to the barn yet?"

"Land, yes!" she answered. "He's been out 'most an hour. Must be about done by now."

Bud hastened through the kitchen. In the shed Tug leaped upon him, whining in a frenzy of delight. It was the first night they had slept apart since the terrier's puppyhood. Together they went on through the dark carriage house and into the barn. Mr. Mason was milking the next to the last cow. He greeted Bud and nodded his head in the direction of the dog. "That's a well-trained pup," he said. "Most young dogs would be jumpin' around barkin' and scarin' the cattle. They're a little nervous having a strange critter around, of course, but he's as sober as a jedge, himself."

"I taught him to behave when we lived in the stable," said Bud, pleased at having the terrier praised. "What can I do, Mr. Mason?"

"Listen," said the farmer. "I'm not a mite used to bein' called that by my family. Remember—it's Uncle John and Aunt Sarah. If you want to help, take a fork an' go up to the top o' the high mow. You can throw down about six forkfuls o' hay."

Bud swarmed up the ladder till he was close under the cobwebby roof. There he stepped off on the springy surface of the mow. He had never seen any hay except the kind that came in bales. He sank his fork in the fragrant clover and sent it down in slithering masses, the first of which half buried the startled Tug, waiting at the foot of the ladder.

When the early chores were finished they went in to breakfast. Sausage and griddle-cakes and real New Hampshire maple syrup! Bud, who had always supposed his appetite had no limits, found he had to stop before the tall stack of buckwheats was entirely gone.

Uncle John pushed back his chair. "All right, youngster," said he, "let's see what there is to do." They went out to the barn and rolled back the big door at the

front. Bright morning sunshine streamed in, lighting the dancing motes of dust.

"Feels pretty warm fer December," said the farmer. "Some o' this snow'll melt off today." He turned the cows into the barnyard, where they drank at the hollowed-out half log that served as a trough. Then, whistling cheerily, he set about cleaning the tie-up.

"Do you want me to take care o' the horse, Uncle John?" Bud asked.

Mr. Mason nodded. "Try it an' see how you make out," he said.

Bud watered the mare and fed her, then raked out the roomy stall. Looking in a box nailed to the wall, he found a currycomb and brush. Old Betsy turned her head to sniff at him as he went in beside her. He patted her shoulder. "Stand still, girl," he said in the gruff voice he had heard the Bull's Head teamsters use. The mare seemed satisfied and went back to her hay. For half an hour Bud toiled over her fat sides, first with the currycomb, then with the brush. It is doubtful if the old sorrel had ever had such a polishing. When it was done her winter coat, long as it was, gleamed with ruddy lights.

Uncle John finished in the tie-up and came to look at the boy's handiwork. "Whew!" he whistled in real surprise. "You *do* know somethin' about horses, don't you? Now come on back in the house. I want to fit you out with an old pair o' rubber boots, so you can go with me out to the sheep pen."

By wearing his own shoes inside them Bud managed to keep the boots on his feet, and they set out along a path trodden in the snow behind the barn. Tug trotted here and there, nosing into corners, examining his new

41

surroundings and finding them good. The sheep pen stood at the edge of an old apple orchard, nearly two hundred yards from the other buildings. A partly demolished haystack stood beside it, and a low, inclosed shed, with its roof built out from the hillside, housed the sheep. When Uncle John pulled open the door they stood huddled and blinking, not seeming to want to come out. The farmer pulled a fork from the stack and began strewing hay in heaps around the pen. Still the sheep stayed inside.

"That's funny," said the farmer. "Here, you silly things, come out to breakfast."

At last, after some urging, an old ewe ventured forth and the others quickly followed.

"Maybe 'twas the dog," mused Uncle John. "Still, he's up back o' the shed, payin' no attention to 'em."

At that moment Tug gave voice to a short, deep bark. Bud saw him standing on the hillside above the shed roof, sniffing at the snow. His rigid legs and the hackles rising along his back were proof of his excitement. "Look! He's found something!" cried the boy. They left the pen and hurried up the slope to the terrier's side.

Uncle John was in the lead. "Wal, I'll be hornswoggled!" he suddenly exclaimed, bending down. "See them tracks, Bud? Must be a bobcat, an' a wallopin' big one. Here's where he scratched down into the shingles. It's a good thing I built that roof stout, or he'd have got in."

42

Bud stared at the deep, round impressions in the snow.

"Gosh!" said he. "How big is a bobcat, Uncle John? Could he kill sheep?"

"Sure could," said the farmer seriously. "That feller'd be about the size o' Tug there, an' all claws an' whiskers an' cussedness. There ain't been one on this side o' the mountain fer years. He won't be back in daylight, so we can leave the sheep out here with their fodder. I'll

have to go 'round the shed an' make sure all the planks are tight before I shut 'em up again."

As they took their way back toward the house, Mr. Mason looked at his watch. "Only ten o'clock," he said. "We might go up in the north pasture an' pick out a Christmas tree. Want to try it, or do your feet hurt in those boots?"

Bud hastened to assure him that the boots were comfortable. They got an ax from the shed and started up the hill. The path twisted among clumps of juniper and skirted ledges for nearly a quarter of a mile. Then of a sudden it plunged into a thicket of bushy young white pines and went up on a steep slant beside an old stone wall. Another three or four hundred yards of climbing, and Uncle John pointed to a different type of evergreen. "Here's where the firs begin," he said, "and the pines start to peter out. There's spruce mixed in with both of 'em, but the real Christmas trees like the high ground best."

He showed Bud how to identify the leaf of the balsam fir by its flat spills with their tiny white stripes underneath.

"I ain't bothered with a tree fer years," he said. "Havin' a boy in the house, though, we'll have to make it a real Christmas this year."

They chose a pretty balsam, seven or eight feet tall, with a top as straight and pointed as a spear. Uncle John cleared a place in the snow at the foot of the tree and with two carefully directed blows of the ax cut it off cleanly, close to the ground.

"Gee, could I carry it?" asked Bud, and swung the tree proudly over his shoulder, holding it by the butt. For all its bushy bulk it was extraordinarily light.

"Feel how soft those tips are?" said Uncle John as they returned down the mountainside. "They make the nicest bed you ever slept on. You an' me'll have to camp out some night, up in the woods. We'll build a pole shelter an' fix us some balsam beds an' then jest roll up in our blankets, front o' the camp fire."

"Gosh!" whispered Bud. And then, after a pause, "Say, do you think you could let me stay here quite a long while? I'll work an' help all I can. Gee, I—I like this the best of any place in the world."

Mr. Mason's head went back in a big laugh. "I guess we can make out to keep you a spell," he said. "Don't you fret yourself about that. Now let's see what it was that smelled so good when I came past the kitchen."

All that day and the next Bud and his dog spent with Uncle John, going about the place, looking after the stock, tending the fires and doing odd bits of work. "If you want to be a real help," said the farmer, "you can bring in the wood fer Aunt Sarah. That'll be your job—to keep the wood-boxes full." And he showed Bud how to stack up the birch and maple sticks on his arm and carry them without spilling.

The day following was market day, and Uncle John hurried through the chores so as to make an early start. The butter was brought up in crocks from the dim, cool regions of the cellar, and carefully packed in a big wooden box with a hinged cover that occupied the rear of the sleigh. By the time the old, slow-ticking clock in the kitchen said eight-thirty the farmer was on his way.

As Aunt Sarah bustled about the kitchen getting her pies ready for the oven, she looked kindly over at Bud.

"Christmas is only three days off," she said. "What do you think you'd like most?"

Bud flushed. "I dunno," he answered. "Once my Pop gave me a pair o' pants. And one Christmas I got a handkerchief and a little stockin' full of candy, at the

45

school. But this year—gee—I can't think of anything more I need, except maybe a collar for Tug—so the cops won't get him."

Aunt Sarah gave a kind of snort. "Well," she said, "you're certainly easy satisfied compared to some boys. We'll see what happens."

The day passed slowly with Uncle John away. Bud

fed the chickens, then carried in armfuls of wood till the boxes fairly overflowed. Finally he went out to the carriage house, climbed into the buggy, and tried to imagine that he was rolling down Commonwealth Avenue behind a stepper. Just as that pastime was beginning to bore him he heard a jingle of sleigh-bells outside. Through the window he saw old Betsy standing in the yard and caught a glimpse of the farmer just vanishing into the house with his arms full of odd-looking bundles.

Bud flung open the big rolling door and led the sorrel mare in out of the cold. For cold it was. No wind stirred, but a biting chill was in the air, damp and raw. The sky, from one horizon to the other, was leaden gray. Even to the city-bred boy, who knew little of the weather and its signs, there was something ominous in the hard still-- ness that had shut down over the mountain.

Soon Uncle John joined him in the barn and helped with the unharnessing. "Shouldn't wonder if we'd git a storm by mornin'," he said, carefully rubbing down the mare's steaming legs with a rough cloth. "We'd better make certain everything's snug an' ship-shape 'fore we go to bed tonight."

Sure enough, by supper time the wind had begun to prowl around the corners of the house, snuffing hungrily at the window-frames and wailing in the chimneys. Bud was glad of the drowsy warmth beside the stove. When the dishes were done he tried to read, but soon his eye- lids began to droop. Good nights were said, and he climbed the stairs, carrying an extra quilt that Aunt Sarah had given him as a precaution against the cold.

The wind was rising steadily, and as he wriggled out of his clothes and into his flannel nightshirt the boy could hear the huge roof timbers of the old house creak and groan in the blast. There was an added sound now—the *shish-shish* of snow particles driven against the shingles. With a bound Bud got into the big old feather bed and snuggled under the covers. Soon he had warmed a place for himself, but with the threatening scream of the gale in his ears, it took him a long while to go to sleep.

He must have dozed off at last, for it was hours later that he was wakened suddenly from an uneasy slumber and found himself sitting bolt upright in bed. A great gust of wind was fairly rocking the house, and he had a dim memory of something like a terrific crash.

Shivering, Bud heard voices and hurried footsteps downstairs, followed by the clump of boots and the kitchen door slamming shut. He pulled the quilt around him and listened intently, but for what seemed a long time nothing happened. At last there came the bang of the door once more, and above the roar of the storm he caught fragments of excited talk.

" . . . Old maple tree, back o' the barn," Uncle John was saying " . . . smashed the lean-to an' the mare's stall all to . . . no, not a sign of her . . . can't do any more till morning." At that point the howling wind drowned out his voice. Bud's teeth chattered. He crawled back into his warm nest and lay wondering about the fate of old Betsy until sleep overtook him once more.

48

V

BY MORNING the storm was over. A deep blanket
of white lay over the world, drifted in places into
huge, grotesque mounds and ridges. Bud hastened downstairs to find Aunt Sarah getting breakfast and Uncle
John already out hunting for traces of the mare.

"He dug up an old pair of snowshoes for you," the
farmer's wife said. "Dress warm an' tie 'em on your feet.
Here—like this," and she showed him how to put the
toes of his boots into the broad straps.

In a few moments the boy was out on the four-foot
crest of a drift beside the shed. Tug tried to accompany
him, but the dog broke through the wind-packed surface
every step or two and had to be pulled out by the collar.

Finally Bud sent him back to the house and went on in the tracks of the farmer. At first he had trouble in keeping his feet. The broad, clumsy shoes seemed bound to interfere with each other. But in a few moments he had mastered the trick of walking wide and made better progress.

At the rear of the barn there was devastation. The silver maple that had stood at the corner of the fenced barnyard lay like a stricken giant, its bare arms thrust upward from the débris of the lean-to. The splintered stump showed a gaping hollow at the heart.

Bud found Uncle John striding in a slow circle around the outer side of the barnyard, pausing every now and then to look closely at the snow. As the boy drew near he seemed to have found what he was seeking. "Here's a place," he said, pointing to a slight depression in the drifted surface. "She might have gone this way."

They went up the hillside twenty yards or more and came to another shallow trough in the snow. "Yep," said the farmer, "I reckon this is what's left of her trail. She must have been up to her belly in snow, poor old lady! 'Twas a miracle she didn't get killed by the tree, an' it'll be another if she ain't froze to death."

They went on in silence, finding an occasional faint trace of the mare's progress. But at the second stone wall, a quarter of a mile from the house, there seemed to be no further signs. After a half hour's fruitless search

Uncle John turned back. "The stock's got to be tended to," he said. "We'll try again, later."

Gloom hung over the breakfast table. Even Aunt Sarah's cheerful voice was silent. As soon as the meal was eaten Uncle John hurried out to the barn and with Bud's help finished the chores. Then he came back to the house and quickly, almost sadly, took the shotgun down from its pegs on the shed wall. "Can't tell," he said. "She might be in bad shape." He loaded it with buckshot shells and slipped a handful into the pockets of his mackinaw. To Bud he handed a rope halter, and together they set out once more on their snowshoes.

When they reached the place where they had lost the trail Uncle John started the boy walking in a wide semicircle to the left, while he himself set out in the opposite direction. Bud plodded on, skirting clumps of sumach and scrub pine and birch, looking everywhere for some break in the wind-packed snow that would tell of the old sorrel's progress. Just as he was thinking that it was hopeless he found himself looking down at a fresh trail. No floundering mare had made this. It was a series of rounded tracks, blurred a little by the sifting of the dry snow, but still showing toe-pugs that indicated their direction. The tracks were a good three inches across and looked like those of a big dog. No—not a dog—a cat.

Curious, Bud turned and followed this trail upward to the left along the hill. And before he had gone fifty yards he realized that under the fresh tracks were other signs—a series of broad depressions, almost obliterated —the wallowing path of old Betsy. He looked again to make sure, then raised his voice in a hail. Uncle John answered down the hill and hurried to his side.

"Well, jest look at that!" he exclaimed. "It's the big bobcat a-followin' the mare's trail, sure's you're born. Come on, sonny!" And with that he set off at a fast pace up the mountain.

With the tracks of the bobcat as a guide they went on for nearly half a mile and reached a wild upland pasture thick with brush and dotted with evergreens of various kinds. It was just as they were skirting a dense clump of cedars that things began to happen all at once.

Uncle John was several paces in the lead. Of a sudden there came a crashing sound among the trees and a sort of half-snort, half-whinny of terror. The next instant a furry gray shape broke cover almost beside them and went bounding over the snow toward another clump of brush. Quick as a flash Uncle John raised his shotgun and fired. As the echo of the report went thundering among the ledges Bud saw the gray animal leap into the air with a convulsive twist of its body and fall, clawing and spitting, in the snow.

The farmer moved toward it cautiously, his gun held ready, and Bud followed close at his heels. He got a glimpse of the creature lying on its side, its round, cat-like head turned toward them. The long ears with tufts of hair at the tips were laid back, and white teeth gleamed in a menacing snarl. Carefully Uncle John took aim once more and fired the second barrel. Then he stepped forward. "It's all right, Buddy," he said. "That finished him. Say, he's a whopper, too. Biggest bobcat I ever saw."

The boy came and looked down. Stretched in the bloody snow, the limp gray body did not look so formidable. He thought the lynx might have been as large as Tug, but it was certainly thinner and lighter in weight. He poked it to make sure it was dead, then took the hind legs in his mittened hands and dragged the animal after him. Uncle John had already hastened back to the clump of cedars. As Bud drew near he heard a startled exclamation from the farmer.

"Great granddaddy fishhooks!" he cried. "Did you ever see such a sight in your life? Bud, come here a-runnin'!"

At once the boy dropped the bobcat and galloped toward the voice as fast as his snowshoes would take him. Coming around a tree he almost ran into Uncle John. There in the shelter of the cedars was a little clear space almost like a room. In the middle, where the snow had been trampled down, stood old Betsy. She was gaunt and disheveled-looking, her shaggy coat gray with snow particles and her mane and foretop fringed with icicles. But there was a gesture of pride in the toss of the head with which she greeted them. And no wonder! For at her side stood a tiny, long-legged mite of a horse—the first newly foaled colt that Bud had ever seen. The little fellow stood there, feet spread to brace him, a look of fearless wonder in his bright baby eyes. His coat was a deep ruddy sorrel that bordered on bay. But the fuzzy little mane between his ears was blond like his mother's.

"You little son-of-a-gun!" chuckled Uncle John. "How in time d' you think we're goin' to get you home?" He stepped forward slowly, his hand held out, and spoke soothingly to the mare.

She stood, trembling a little as he stroked her neck, then nuzzled coyly at his pocket. And sure enough, he pulled out a lump of sugar, put there for just such an occasion.

Then he turned to the foal. Stooping, he lifted the ungainly little fellow in both his arms, while the mare watched him anxiously. At a slow pace, talking gently all the time, he started for home. It was slow going, for the colt was an awkward load. The mother floundered along in his wake as best she could, striving to keep her nose within six inches of Uncle John's elbow. Bud brought up the rear, carrying the gun and the unneeded halter. He had decided to leave the body of the gray prowler for a later trip.

After many rests, the little procession descended the final slope into the barnyard, and in answer to a great shout from Uncle John, Aunt Sarah came open-mouthed to the kitchen window. As they rolled back the big door and entered the warm dusk of the barn she came rushing out to greet them, a shawl thrown hastily about her shoulders.

"My lands!" she cried. "Did you ever see the beat o' that, now? A colt! An' say, if he ain't a little beauty, too!"

While her husband placed some boards to make a temporary box-stall at the end of the barn floor, Aunt Sarah rubbed down the wet, heaving sides of the mare with a burlap bag, and Bud brought pails of water from which old Betsy drank long and eagerly.

When at last she and her baby were ensconced in their new quarters, the boy strapped on his snowshoes and climbed the hill once more. Half dragging, half carrying, he managed to bring home the stiffened body of the lynx. Uncle John saw him coming and grinned. "You must be aimin' to have a fur coat," said he. They laid the dead bobcat on a plank and proceeded to skin it while Tug looked on with breathless interest. By the time dinner was ready they had nailed the mottled gray hide to the shed door.

It was while they were putting the finishing touches on the new stall that afternoon that Uncle John laughed suddenly and struck his thigh a resounding whack. "I've got it," he said—"a name for the colt. He sure is a tough little feller an' no 'mount o' weather seems to hurt him. Then with that pretty red color o' his, an' the clump o' trees his ma picked to have him born in, there's just one thing to call him—Cedar. Look at him now—see him whisk that little brush of a tail while he goes after his dinner! Cussed if he ain't a smart youngster!"

Uncle John paused and straightened up, the hammer in his hand. "You know, Bud," he said, nodding emphatically, "that baby's goin' to make a horse! I'll tell you about it. Back about seven years ago there was a big match race billed down at Granite State Park. I remember it was a hot, dusty day in the fall. All summer on the county tracks Bill Brady's black mare, Kitty B., had been cleanin' up the stakes. She was as pretty a trotter as I ever saw—nervous but lightnin'-fast. She was ready for the Grand Circuit right then, but her owner figgered he could win more money with her up here in the sticks. She'd done 2.06 an' all the local sports believed she'd beat that time if she was pushed.

"Then in September a Nashua man named Loomis brought a big young stallion over from Vermont for the fall meetin's. They called him Caribou, and he was a natural pacer.

"This horse had been gettin' his first racin' at the up-country fairs and the story was he'd never lost a heat. Folks believed it after he'd won his first three starts in New Hampshire, an' when his owner challenged Brady to a match race on the mile track a lot of us hereabouts decided to be there.

"Before the race there was a big crowd around Kitty B.'s stall an' 'most as many lookin' over the Vermont stallion. My, but he was a horse! He stood up, big an' high-headed, with his bright bay coat shinin', an' the odds begun to drop to even money after the wise ones got a good look at him.

"This race was to be run in three heats. Brady got the mare away to a beautiful start in the first an' held the pole. On the back stretch Caribou begun to come up fast, and he was right by her wheels around the last turn. There never was a better driver than Bill Brady, an' he managed to bring the mare in, under the whip, just a nose ahead at the wire. The time was 2.05¼.

"Kitty B. was still lathered and jumpy when she came up for the second heat, and spite of all Brady could do the pacer cut in ahead of her an' took the pole as they passed the half-mile post. Boy, how he come down that stretch! No whippin'. Just that natural, long pacin' stride eatin' up the track. Brady tried hard, but the mare didn't have a look-in. You should have heard the crowd cheer when the time went up—2.04! An' that big horse was only gettin' started.

"There was a good long rest before the third heat, an' Kitty B. came back fairly fresh. Brady took her away fast an' she got on the pole, trottin' for all she was worth. Caribou crept up, inch by inch, till he was half a length ahead, but still she kept the pole. That's the way they fought, all the way up the back stretch. Caribou's driver swung him wide on the last turn, an' he struck a patch of rough goin' where the track hadn't been dragged.

57

Must have stepped on a clod, for he stumbled. He was
back in his stride in a second an' came down to the finish
with everything he had—everything but the old speed.
They were neck an' neck as they went under the wire—
so close the judges called for a new heat. But Caribou
didn't race again that day or any day. That stumble had
finished him for the track. He pulled up dead lame in
front."

Uncle John pulled a spear of timothy out of the hay-
mow and chewed it reflectively. Bud had been listening,
never taking his eyes from the farmer's face. The half-
familiar jargon of the harness track sent little prickles
of excitement running up and down his spine.

"I've watched a heap o' horses," Uncle John continued
at length, "but none that could touch Caribou fer speed
an' courage. Ever since the day o' that race I've wanted
to own one of his colts, an' now I've got one. Ol' Betsy's
never been on a track, but she can do her ten miles an
hour on the road all day long. So I'm hopin' that little
Cedar here is goin' to grow up a credit to both his daddy
an' his ma.

"Wal," he finished, and his eyes twinkled back at the
boy's, "you pick up the hammer, Bud, and we'll mosey
along. It's gittin' dusk. Time to light the lanterns an'
feed the stock."

VI

BUD'S first Christmas Eve on Red Horse Hill came, cold and clear, with a sharp-edged sliver of a moon lighting the western sky. All day Aunt Sarah had been bustling mysteriously about the kitchen, shooing the boy out whenever the tantalizing smells of her cooking brought him near.

With Uncle John away at town meeting in the village, Bud had taken the white bull terrier and gone on another of his explorations. A warm sun had melted the surface of the drifts, and a cold night had made a firm crust over all the landscape. It bore Tug's weight with ease, and even Bud found snowshoes unnecessary. They had gone sliding and scrambling far down the hill to the brook that drained the lower meadow, and there, while Bud was bending down to hear the soft cluck of the water under the ice, the dog had made a discovery. His sudden bark brought his master to his side. There, under an overhanging shelf of the snow, the boy found a hole in the bank just above the level of the ice. It was about the size of his arm and seemed to extend upward into the earth. In the snow beneath it was a faint trail, leading off along the sheltered bank. Bud studied it carefully but could pick out no track clear enough to give him an idea of the animal that had made it.

That evening he told Uncle John about his discovery. "Good enough!" exclaimed the farmer. "I knew there was muskrats down there in the old days, but nobody's trapped 'em for years. Likely by now they've got plentiful. Wal, we'll see 'bout that later. It's time fer you to be in bed now if you're agoin' to wake up early enough fer tomorrow's big doin's."

Bud heard the elders moving about the dining-room long after he had crawled under the covers. There were rustling noises that sounded like paper, and queer bumpings on the floor and smothered laughter from Uncle John. Finally, however hard he tried to listen, the boy could keep awake no longer. The next sound he heard was the dawn-challenging bugle call of Miles Standish, the big Plymouth Rock rooster.

The instant Bud realized that it was Christmas morning he jumped out of bed. In record time he pulled on his clothes, and taking his shoes in one hand, tiptoed down the stairs. It was still dark, and for once the farmer

and his wife seemed to have overslept. No noise of break-
fast-getting came from the kitchen. Bud stood a moment
listening. Then as his eyes roved about the room he gave
a sudden gasp. In the far corner stood a tree—his balsam
—transformed with gleaming tinsel balls and festooned
with strings of popcorn. Tucked in its branches and lying on the floor beneath it were packages of alluring
shapes.

"Gee whillikens!" he breathed and stepped closer,
peering down at an object half concealed by the lower
branches. Could it be—it was—a sled! Bud was unable
to restrain himself longer. He let out a whoop of joy.
And at that second the kitchen door opened.

"Merry Christmas!" shouted Uncle John and Aunt
Sarah together.

They waited until after breakfast to open the gifts.
Then Tug was brought in, grinning from ear to ear, to
share in the fun. One by one, Uncle John took the packages from under the tree and handed them to the proper
parties. At first the gifts came in regular rotation, but
soon the elders and Tug dropped out, and Bud sat alone,
opening package after package. There were new fleece-
lined leather mittens, and shoes, and high buckled rubbers
like Uncle John's. There was a neat gray suit of clothes,
a mackinaw, cap, stockings, underwear, shirts. The beautiful sled with its wooden sides and polished spring
runners came next. On its red painted top was a name
done in flowing letters—Dan Patch.

" 'Ever hear o' him?'' asked the farmer, his eyes twinkling.

"Yes, sir!" cried Bud. "World's champion pacing horse. They had his picture in the office at the Bull's Head."

There was one more package, bulky and heavy, that clanked when Uncle John laid it in Bud's lap. As he untied the wrapper half a dozen odd-shaped steel contrivances appeared, in a tangle of chains.

"There!" exclaimed Uncle John. "Now we can get acquainted with those muskrats, down along the brook! Six Number One jump traps. We'll set 'em this afternoon."

Two of the packages were marked for Tug. One held a handsome collar with brass studs and name plate. The other was a box of dog biscuit.

Bud, who had never known such a Christmas in all his life, sat in the middle of the floor among his gifts, trying to swallow the lump in his throat. And Uncle John must have felt somewhat the same way, for his voice was husky as he said, "All right, sonny, let's tackle the chores."

That was a day to be remembered. In the afternoon Bud tried out the new sled on a long, smooth sweep of crust, and for a quarter of a mile he flew faster than the great Dan Patch had ever paced. Later they visited the lower meadow. Uncle John showed Bud how to place his traps under the holes in the bank with dry snow sprinkled over them and a heavy wooden clog at the end of each chain.

In the days that followed Bud spent much of his time along the trap line. He tried various methods of setting and experimented with a number of kinds of bait, including corn meal and strips of meat, but the most successful sets were made with empty traps hidden in the animals' paths. At the end of two weeks the brook seemed pretty well cleaned out and the boy had twelve muskrats and two mink to show for his efforts. Uncle John had shown him how to strip the skins off over the head and stretch them on frames whittled out of pieces of shingle. When they were dry the farmer took them to a fur buyer in Riverdale who gave him eighteen dollars for the lot. The following market day he and Bud visited the bank, and the boy proudly deposited his money in a savings account.

Bud made rapid progress at learning to milk. He had strong hands and a natural gentleness with animals. Within a week of the time he had his first lesson he was allowed to milk two of the older cows night and morning. It was on an evening in the first week of the new year, when they were carrying in the milk from the barn, that Uncle John brought up a new and disturbing subject.

"Meadow Hill School opens up for the winter term tomorrow," he said. "Now you've got clothes an' everything you need, you'll be wantin' to go."

For a moment panic seized Bud. He hated school instinctively. His first thought was to take Tug and run away—it didn't matter where—anywhere, so long as he stayed free. But as they entered the warm lamplit kitchen and Uncle John's kindly voice continued, a different feeling came to him. This was home—the first home he had had since he was a little boy. He would stay, school or no school.

"Miss Carson's a mighty good teacher," the farmer was saying. "You'll get along fine, I expect."

Next morning Aunt Sarah brushed Bud's hair with her own hands and gave his neck and ears an even more thorough inspection than usual. Dressed in his new clothes and wearing a red woolen muffler and mittens knitted by the farmer's wife, Bud was ready to start at eight o'clock. Aunt Sarah had put up a lunch for him and packed it in a clean lard pail. Uncle John came in from the barn. "I'll go with you, this first mornin'," he said, "an' show you where it is."

They went down the road to the foot of the second hill and turned up a fork to the right. They passed three or four farms and then, under a huge sugar maple tree, they saw the schoolhouse. It was very different from the many-windowed brick buildings that Bud had known in Boston—a little white-painted frame structure with two doors in front and a curl of fragrant wood-smoke coming from the chimney. In the middle of the snow-covered yard a flagpole stood.

They entered the nearer door and found themselves in

HE WAS ALLOWED TO MILK TWO OF THE OLDER COWS

a narrow vestibule running across the front of the building, its walls lined with coat hooks. Beyond, two more doors opened into the schoolroom itself. Just inside, a big sheet-iron stove crackled cheerfully, and the woodbox behind it was piled high with maple and birch. There were windows at both sides of the room, and the rows of benches faced the teacher's desk which stood on a low platform at the farther end. Miss Carson turned from the blackboard and came down to meet them. From the moment Bud saw her he decided that school might be bearable after all.

She was a middle-aged woman with graying hair and strong, capable hands. Her blue eyes held a twinkle of humor.

"Hartley Martin?" she asked. "I've heard about you and hoped you'd be coming to school. If you don't mind I'll call you Bud. What grade were you in at your last school, Bud?"

Uncle John stood by to lend him moral support while he battled through a page in the Sixth Reader, then left him adding up a column of figures.

Soon the other pupils began to arrive. There were thirty-five of them in all, ranging from tots of five and six to strapping farm lads of fourteen. Bud was placed temporarily among the seventh-graders. He shared a desk in the next to the last row with a chunky towheaded boy named Calvin Hunter, who looked him over with a cool, appraising eye and made no advances.

There was a "short recess" at ten-thirty and a "long recess" of forty-five minutes at noon. The boys and girls who lived near enough went home to dinner. The rest gobbled their lunches and ran out to play. The snow lay a foot deep and more in the schoolyard and while the girls trod out a circle for "fox and geese," the boys began pushing up mountainous rolls of snow and building a fort.

Bud was the last to finish his sandwiches and pie. He pulled on his cap and was just starting down the steps when a snowball whizzed past his head and broke against the clapboard wall with a thud.

A gleam came into Bud's eye. This was the sort of reception he was used to. He cast a quick glance about the yard, stuffed his mittens in his pocket, and jumped down into the snow beside the steps.

"City kid! City kid! Knock his cap off!" came a chorus of gleeful shouts, and another white missile came sailing toward him. Bud dodged and scooped up a double handful of snow in the same motion. His watchful eyes never left the enemy as he slapped his snowball deftly into shape and tucked it beneath his elbow. He was under a heavy fire now from half a dozen points. Shifting quickly he ducked and sidestepped until two more snowballs lay in the crook of his arm. Then he took the offensive.

The boys saw him take a step forward, and those who still had snowballs redoubled their bombardment. The rest started for cover. As one of them was scrambling over the wall of the half-finished fort, Bud sent a stinging liner to the seat of his breeches that brought forth a yelp of anguish. Some of the hostile forces paused to guffaw at this, but Bud was in grim earnest. His second snowball carried away the cap of one of the loudest laughers. And his third landed so hard in the midsection of a tall, lanky farmer's boy that he doubled up and sat down in the snow.

Cal Hunter gave a cheer of triumph as he saw the last of Bud's ammunition used up. He had saved his hardest-packed "water-soaker" for this opportunity, and now he let it drive with all his strength and an excellent aim. Bud did not dodge. He put up his bare hands, caught the snowball, and whipped it back like a flash. Almost before Cal knew what was happening the heavy water-soaker smote him on the ear, knocking him backward into a drift.

Bud crossed the yard and stood in front of the stocky country boy as he got dizzily to his feet. He expected a fight and was ready for it. But as the towhead faced him a grin overspread his ruddy face. "Jumpin' gee whillikers," he gurgled, "that was a beaut' of a shot!"

He turned to the others. "Maybe he's a city kid," said Cal, "but him and me'll stand the hull kaboodle of ye in a snowfight soon's the fort's ready."

VII

AFTER that first noon recess Bud's standing among his schoolmates was assured. The respect inspired by his marksmanship saved him from any further teasing. They asked him about the sights of Boston and listened in rapt attention while he described them. In return they expounded the lore of the backwoods. And even when he failed to understand some fact that was common knowledge to every country boy they explained it to him without taunting him with his ignorance.

With Cal Hunter he formed a lasting alliance. Cal lived on a farm a mile down the road from Red Horse Hill. His father, Myron Hunter, owned four pairs of horses and hauled cordwood to town during the winter months. In the long sheds behind his barn half a dozen big two-horse "bobs" were kept—roughly built racks with a stout home-made sled under each end.

Mr. Hunter's teamsters were young French Canadians, Leo, Aristide, and Gideon by name, who had a shack of their own up on the mountain and came singing past the house every morning at daybreak on their way to work.

As often as he was able Bud went down to the Hunter farm after school to play with Cal and to help with the unharnessing when the steaming teams came in from work. These horses were different from the big western-bred drafters he had known in the city. Three of the teams were of a breed called "Canada chunks"—tough, sturdy animals brought down from Quebec for work in the woods. The other pair were New Hampshire bred. Bess and Major were their names and they were red roans, big-boned but fast and clever on their feet. When the loaded sleds started down the mountain this team was always given the lead. According to Cal they could outwalk and outpull any team in the county, and with the big roans setting the pace the string of sleds reached Riverdale in three hours or better.

The Hunters also kept a yoke of oxen for work on the farm and in the thick brush. They were great, sleek brutes with amazing power in their short legs and supple bodies. They were named Star and Golden, and with oxen names are important, for they are driven almost entirely by words of command. Bud fairly gasped the first time he saw them snaking a huge hemlock log out of the woods with no more harness than a big ox-chain hooked to the ring of the heavy wooden yoke across their necks. In perfect obedience to Mr. Hunter's voice they moved forward, pulling to right or left with slow, ponderous strides. "Hup!" he would call. "Gee, there, Star! Haw, Golden!" He walked by the head of the "nigh" ox—the left-hand

71

member of the team. The goad, a straight, slim piece of ash, about the size of a billiard cue, he touched lightly across their shoulders or noses, constantly guiding and urging them. Only in an occasional emergency did he use the sharp brad in the end of the goad to prod them on.

Star was a black and white ox with a four-pointed white spot in the middle of his forehead. He was as gentle

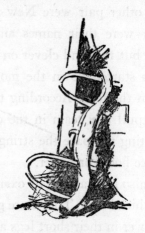

and even-tempered as a lamb. Golden was jet black from nose to tail, and there was a restless spark in his eye. He was inclined to paw and toss his head when things did not suit him. Both had long, smooth-curving horns, tipped with knobs of brass.

Cal owned a pair of red steers, yearlings, that he was training. On Saturdays when Bud could get off to visit his friend they would spend the whole day "geeing" and "hawing" the little fellows up and down the yard, with one boy driving and the other riding the light stone-boat

THEY WOULD SPEND THE WHOLE DAY "GEEING" AND "HAWING"

to which the steers were hitched. Cal himself had chopped and whittled a small yoke for them, curving it to fit their necks. The bows were of hickory, bent while they were green and held in shape until they seasoned.

It would take a bigger book than this to list the hun-

dreds of things that Bud learned that winter. Every day he acquired new skill. He learned to handle an ax like a veteran, for he helped Uncle John get out cord after cord of hardwood for the next year's fires. He learned too how to care for his tools, sharpening the axes to a keen, biting edge on the big grindstone in the shed. He learned to mend harness and gained a deal of knowledge about rough and ready farm carpentry.

As spring came on there were even more things to be

done about the farm. Lambing-time brought much activity around the sheep-pen and some of the lambs had to be nursed from a bottle and warmed by the kitchen stove. In late February and early March the sap was running in the sugar maples, and Bud learned how to tap trees. When the sap was gathered in brimming pails it was his duty to keep the fires hot under the sap-kettles. And when the sugar was finally ready he did his share in eating it.

By the time the spring plowing and planting were over Bud had filled out, broad and hard. He was two inches taller than when he came to the farm and twelve pounds heavier—as tanned and husky as any boy on the mountain. He was not the only member of the farm family who had grown. Cedar, the colt, had shot up like a weed. His long legs were even longer and his ridiculous little body had taken shape in a round, red barrel, clean and trim, with a deep chest and a sturdy rump.

In April Uncle John bought another horse, an eight-year-old gelding called Prince, strong and willing, but without any claims to speed on the road. He did the bulk of the spring work, pulling with old Betsy in double harness when a two-horse team was necessary. For the most part the sorrel mare ran loose with her colt in the barn lot.

Tug, too, was growing used to the farm. He followed his master everywhere and during school hours roamed the woods and fields on the south side of Blue Job till he knew every fox hole and woodchuck burrow. That summer while Bud hoed, pulled weeds, or worked in the hay field the dog kept him company. And on days when Uncle John did not need his help he and Tug went roving together. The terrier accepted Cal Hunter as the friend of his master, but when the stocky farmer's boy attempted to give him orders Tug gently ignored them. He was a one-man dog like all of his breed. Cal's frisky collie, Shep, after one disastrous attempt at a quarrel, was glad to have the white terrier for a comrade.

The two boys and their dogs covered many leagues of country that summer. They found a swimming-hole in a quiet reach below the rapids of Mad River, and thither they repaired on hot afternoons. At other times they made miserable the lives of the woodchucks on Red Horse Hill. Once the beast that the dogs ran to earth turned out to be black and white instead of brown, and that evening Bud had to burn a good pair of overalls, while Tug was allowed no nearer the house than the pig-pen.

Following the potato digging and before the corn was ready to cut for the silo, there came bright fall days when Cal oiled his .22-caliber rifle and showed Bud how to shoot. The city boy had a keen eye and a steady hand. By the time he had used up two or three boxes of shorts in target practice on trees and tin cans he could hold his own successfully with Cal. From that time on they carried the rifle by turns and took alternate shots at any game they saw.

It was the season of the year when bluejays rioted in the beech and hickory groves, jeering at the busy squirrels. Jays were commonly regarded as notorious criminals, and the boys considered them fair game. They were hard to shoot, too—always on the move and always screened from the hunter by thick foliage. Bud and Cal started stalking a flock of the birds one afternoon and followed them southward from one clump of trees to another, lured forward by their raucous screaming and an occasional glimpse of vivid color between the autumn leaves. The boys were moving through a beech clump on the slope of Hogback Mountain, miles from home, when Bud heard the loud "Thief! Thief!" of a jay, and caught a flash of blue, flitting high among the trees. As he hurried forward with the rifle held ready a sudden thunder of wings right at his feet startled him. A ruffed grouse whirred away from its dusting-place under the beeches and lit in a pine tree fifty yards ahead.

"Gosh!" breathed Cal. "A pa'tridge! See him? Right there in that pine! Quick—take yer shot or else gimme the rifle!"

Bud found the little gray-brown spot in the tree and centered the bead squarely on it. He lifted the barrel a hair's breadth to allow for distance—then fired. The bird rose with a flutter and flew a little way, then went tumbling earthward. "You got him!" yelled Cal, in triumph.

"Must have fallen right in the road," panted Bud as he raced forward. They reached the roadside together, and the first thing that met their eyes was the partridge. It dangled from the fist of a man who had just picked it up—a big man, expensively dressed, whose puffy purple jowls seemed oddly familiar to Bud. He was standing at the edge of the road nearer the boys. Behind him was a huge yellow racing-car of a foreign make, its mammoth hood ending in a shiny brass radiator-shell that jutted out like the prow of a ship. And in the car sat a pudgy, pale-faced boy, whose scowling countenance Bud recognized instantly. It was the youth whose Airedale had made memorable Tug's first morning in New Hampshire. The dog seemed to remember him, too, for there was a steady, low rumble in his throat as he stood at Bud's side.

The man looked up, startled, when the boys appeared, then frowned and swelled out his chest. "Well, what do *you* want?" he blustered

Bud's throat felt dry. "Guess I want that partridge," he said.

"You do, eh?" snorted the man. "Why, that's ridiculous. You were trespassing on my company's property. Don't you know the Northeastern Lumber Company owns the timber rights to all these woods on this side of the mountain? I ought to take you before the sheriff!"

"Listen," said Cal. "Your company don't own *all* the timber rights by a long shot, 'cause my paw owns a couple of wood lots here himself. An' even if you did, you can't keep hunters out unless you post 'No gunnin' ' signs. That's our bird, an' you know it."

The man stared, then laughed loudly. "Foolishness!" he remarked and turned toward the car, still clutching the dead grouse. Bud's ire rose. "Hold him, Tug," he breathed, and suddenly the man stopped. In front of him, grim lips but an inch or two from the crease of his trousers, was the big white terrier. The man hesitated, then took a hasty step backward. This was no dog to trifle with. Tug had grown during the summer. Behind his formidable jaws were sixty pounds of whalebone and courage.

"Will the brute bite?" asked the man, retreating still farther.

"If I let him, Mr. Felton," said Bud, "he'd take the pants right off you."

At the sound of his name Felton turned to stare at the boy who had used it. The faint rumble in Tug's throat swelled to a growl, deep and businesslike, and the man involuntarily backed up once more. "Here," he cried angrily, "take your partridge. Now will you call off that dog and let me get to my car?"

At a word from Bud the terrier reluctantly left his post and trotted back to his master's side. Felton threw down the dead grouse and spun the crank of the great yellow car. As the engine came to life he climbed into the driver's seat. Then his voice reached them above the roar of the exhaust. "I'll settle with you later for this!" he snarled, and letting in his clutch, he nearly ran them down with a vicious swerve of the wheel.

When the smoke and dust of his departure had cleared, the two boys looked at each other and grinned. "You sure put it over him that time!" said Cal. "But he meant what he said. That guy never gits over a grudge. Here, the pa'tridge is yours. I'll carry the rifle."

As they walked back along the ridge Cal pointed westward across a broad sweep of heavily-wooded country. "Felton's right about their company buyin' up timber all through this section," said he. "I guess they aim to start cuttin' next year. See that valley down there a little ways? That's where the Caterwaul runs."

"Caterwaul River?" asked Bud. "Say, we must be close to Silas Hartley's old place, aren't we? He was my grandfather, you know."

"I ain't sure," replied Cal, "but I think I've heard Paw say the Hartley place was way back in the woods there where you see the big stand o' pine. That's some o' the finest timber in the state."

"Let's come back sometime and explore it," said Bud. "Gee, I'd like to see the Caterwaul River close to and maybe find where the old house used to stand. My ma lived there when she was a girl."

Cal was enthusiastic. "Sure," he answered. "We could bring along some bacon an' 'taters an' build a fire to cook 'em."

Several times in the days that followed the boys talked about the trip, but for that fall at least, their plans did not materialize. The autumn work and preparations for

81

winter took all their Saturdays. And Bud was putting extra time on his lessons, for Miss Carson had told him he would be ready to start high school along with Cal after the Christmas holidays. School had begun to mean something to him. He had formed a determination to go through high school and then to college, working his way. So every evening he sat down at the dining-room table and pored over his history, geography, and arithmetic by the light of a big oil lamp.

One night he looked up from his books at the sound of a soft swishing against the window-pane, and it was snowing. The long grip of winter had shut down over the New Hampshire hills.

VIII

ON A day in January the town school barge stopped at the Four Corners, just below Cal Hunter's house, and Bud and Cal climbed the rickety steps at the rear to stumble bashfully over the feet of the boys and girls who already occupied it. The barge was a tall, van-like conveyance with benches along either side and straw scattered on the floor. Drawn by two bony horses, it served as transport for the fifteen youngsters of the mountain township who went to school at Riverdale High.

Cal and Bud registered in the principal's office and were assigned to a classroom. At noon they took their lunch boxes to the basement, where a rough sort of dining-table was provided for pupils from the outlying districts. When school was out, at three, the barge returned on creaking runners to take them home. They left in the morning just at daybreak, and it was dark again before they reached Red Horse Hill.

Wednesday afternoons were an exception. Wednesday was market day, when Uncle John drove down to deliver his butter. He was hardly ever ready to leave until four o'clock, and Bud and Cal had an opportunity to see the sights of the town before meeting him at the square for the ride home.

Good sleighing had prevailed ever since Thanksgiving that year. The speedway, a mile and a half of straight,

level road at the north end of the town, had been packed hard and smooth by weeks of use. And every fair afternoon the fastest horses in Riverdale were brought there for exercise. The moment school was over on Wednesdays Bud and Cal would pull on their coats and make a dash for the speedway.

The city boy had had a glimpse of harness racing that summer at the county fair and had got a tremendous thrill out of it. But that experience was nothing compared to the tingling excitement he felt when he first saw the trotters come flying down the snow path.

In and about Riverdale there were perhaps fifty horses that could step a mile in 2.30 or better. Every man who made any pretensions to wealth owned at least one fast road horse. And the winter speedway was the testing-ground where differences of opinion were settled. The trim cutters, shining black, red, or blue, would go jogging slowly up the track, the drivers chaffing each other, the eager horses prancing a little and snorting in the cold.

A constant musical chime of bells made a background for all other sounds.

At the head of the stretch the sleighs turned. By twos and threes or half a dozen at a time they got under way, picking up speed as they neared the mile post. And then, with a swift thud of hoofs that grew louder moment by moment, the racers came flashing down the white, hard path of snow—horses fighting for the lead, their nostrils flaring wide in the frosty air; fur-coated drivers leaning forward, tense and alert, ready to ply the whip as they neared the finish line.

The boys had watched several of these impromptu brushes when Cal pointed suddenly toward the lower end of the speedway. "Jiminy gosh!" he said. "Here comes one that'll show her heels to all of 'em. See that sulky sleigh with the blue roan trotter? That's Sam Felton's new mare Chocorua. She won the Double Eagle Stakes last year, an' her track record is somewhere down around 2.06 or 2.07. Look at her! Ain't she a beauty?"

Bud had an instinctive dislike for anything belonging to the Feltons, but in spite of himself he had to admire the slim, clipped legs of the slate-colored mare and the smooth grace of her gait as she jogged nearer. Her driver was a grim-faced, grizzled little man in a huge black fur cap, who was gripping a cigar in one corner of his mouth and talking out of the other to the driver of a black and yellow cutter.

"That's Andy Blake, Felton's trainer," said Cal. "Did you hear what he said? He's goin' to give the other hoss a start as fur's the second light pole. An' they've got ten dollars on it. Oh, boy! Now we'll see some fun."

Chocorua's rival was a big brown pacer with a jerky, racking stride. He wore an elaborate set of hobbles and his ears went forward and back uncertainly.

The two sleighs drew slowly away until at the head of the speedway they were hardly more than specks. "There, they're pullin' around now," said Cal at last. The track was clear. They could see the brown horse settle to business and come pounding down the road to the sharp, staccato jingle of the sleigh-bells. A moment later Blake let the mare out after him. Even at that distance the boys could catch the swift flash of her legs and sense her speed.

She had made up all but a dozen yards of the pacer's handicap before the halfway mark was reached. And as she sped past the spot where the boys stood she was gaining at every stride. The picture of the lean roan mare creeping up on the brown horse's flank photographed itself on Bud's retina so clearly that he remembered it long afterward. There was a concentrated fury in her trotting —a look about her wicked, snakelike head with its laid-back ears—that made him shudder even while he admired her speed.

"Golly whiskers!" breathed Cal. "Look at that lady go! There——she's got him. See that? He's goin' to break!"

Sure enough, the pacer wavered in his stride as she took the lead. His rump heaved awkwardly, and he went into a wild, loose-jointed gallop. The ignominious finish of the brush was greeted with a chorus of laughter by the horsemen returning along the sides of the snow path.

"Well," said Cal, as they started down toward the square, "that feller will sure know better'n to bet with Blake again. My paw says this Chocorua's the fastest thing in New England. They didn't know how she'd go on snow, but if anybody asks me, I'll tell 'em!"

That was the first of many glimpses the boys had of the famous blue roan trotter. She had few opportunities to test her speed against the other horses, for most of the drivers were wary of entering into any competition with her. But Blake had her out for exercise nearly every day and usually ended up by trotting her a mile in fast time.

Bud watched every move of the various drivers with

eyes that missed nothing. He could tell almost to a second when a man would begin to use the whip. He figured out for himself why it was that some of the older men were always half a length back until the three-quarter mark and then put on a spurt to win, while less experienced drivers pushed their nags at top speed from the start. He saw tricks tried—sometimes successfully. There was no opportunity to jockey for the pole on the straight-away course, but when several horses were racing there were frequent attempts at boxing. If a fast trotter happened to be behind the leading sleigh, another driver would come up on the outside and keep his nag's head so close to the side of the cutter in front that there was no room for the speedier horse to get through. And once Bud watched a driver in a two-horse heat whip his pacer to a slight lead and then force his rival over into the rough going on the outside of the track.

Each Wednesday night on the drive home Bud and Cal would discuss with Uncle John the brushes they had seen. He was a wise horseman and had driven many impromptu races himself in his younger days. Often he was able to tell Bud why some driver had tried a particular piece of strategy. And always he would wind up the conversation with a chuckle and say, "All right, boys, but just you wait till the red colt gits out there on the snow path! Another year, an' he'll be ready to race."

Cedar, a two-year-old now, according to horse age, was as tall as his mother and as full of life as a kitten. He was broken to lead with a halter, and Uncle John had even accustomed him to the feel of a bit and bridle.

Every Saturday it was Bud's pleasant duty to curry the colt's smooth sides until they gleamed like ruddy mirrors. Old Betsy had long since been moved back into an ordinary stall, and the roomy box-stall had been turned over to her handsome son. Tug, who was allowed the run of the place during the day, was a frequent visitor to Cedar's quarters. They were on the best of terms, and the big white dog liked nothing better than to pick a clean corner of the stall and lie there quietly while the fidgety colt munched his clover.

That was a long, hard winter even for New Hampshire. Storm followed storm, and the snow and freezing weather lasted until late March. It seemed extra long to Bud because he had so little time to himself. He enjoyed going to high school, but the long, tedious hours in the barge were hard to stand. He got home just in time to help with the chores. After that he ate supper, did his school work, and tumbled into bed. He was restless for vacation time and the free, outdoor days of summer.

The cold weather broke at last. There came nights when the sun was still in sight as he climbed Red Horse Hill; when the frogs sang in shrill chorus from the meadow, and the mild air held a languid feel of spring.

It was on such an evening that Bud trudged up the muddy mile of road from Hunter's farm and found a strange horse and buggy standing in the yard. There was something so disreputable and yet so rakishly picturesque about the rig that the boy dropped his books on the door-step and stood a moment looking it over.

The buggy had been a fashionable vehicle in its day. Through the caked mud an occasional spot of red paint still showed on the spokes of the wheels. The top, tilted back at an angle of forty-five degrees, had collapsed entirely on the left side and leaned crazily like a slouch hat worn too far over one eye.

Between the shafts stood a little bay mare, one hip drooping wearily and head hung low. Bud looked at her a second time before he realized that she was no ordinary piece of horseflesh. In spite of the mud that clung to her fetlocks, her legs were trim and well muscled, and her tired head was beautifully proportioned. Some one had driven her far and fast that day. Bud looked around for her owner and for the first time heard voices coming from the barn.

He went into the house and greeted Aunt Sarah, then went out through the shed. Uncle John was standing, fork in hand, by the foot of the ladder. And leaning lazily back against the hay-mow, hands in pockets, stood a stranger. He was of medium height, lithe and muscular in build. A slouch hat, tipped back carelessly on his head, showed a mop of jet-black curly hair. His swarthy complexion gave him a queer, foreign look, yet Bud was at a loss to place his nationality. Not French nor Italian, he thought. The man wore loose-fitting corduroy trousers

"ALL RIGHT," HE SAID. "I WON'T BOTHER YOU NO MORE FOR
A WHILE"

and an old blue jersey tucked inside his belt. From the fringes of his raven curls gleamed small gold earrings.

"So, that bein' the case," Uncle John was saying, "I'm not in need of any help this spring an' don't expect to be later on." He turned and went up the ladder to the top of the mow.

The stranger made no reply, but after a moment he straightened up with a lazily graceful motion and strolled across the barn floor toward Cedar's stall. For the first time Bud noticed Tug. The terrier had been standing perfectly still beside the hay-mow, a half dozen feet from the dark man. Now he walked quietly after him on alert toes, his tail quite motionless and his gaze fixed on the stranger's legs.

While Uncle John was throwing down the evening's fodder the man stood studying Cedar, his piercing black eyes taking in every detail of the sorrel colt's build. At the instant when the farmer started down the ladder once more, his visitor swung quickly away from the stall and sauntered back toward the middle of the floor.

His brown, hawk-featured face wore a masklike smile. "All right," he said. "I won't bother you no more for a while. Do you know any other place might want a man?" He had a deep, soft voice like the purr of a cat, and his accent was unlike any Bud had ever heard.

"No," said Uncle John shortly and went about feeding the stock. The man gave him an odd look, then turned and walked out the partly opened barn door. A moment later Bud caught the sound of buggy wheels and the clink of the little mare's hoofs as the stranger went out of the yard.

The boy came out of the shadow of the carriage-house doorway where he had stood during the conversation. He pulled on his overalls and got his milking-stool.

"Who was that, Uncle John?" he asked as he entered the tie-up.

"Some sort of a gypsy feller," said the farmer. "I never saw him before. He was lookin' fer a job. Said his name was Harko Dan. I didn't care fer his looks much."

Harko Dan. The queer name kept running through Bud's thoughts as he milked, interrupted his home work, and was still repeating itself in his brain as he lay in bed. Somehow he had a feeling that the black-haired gypsy with the little bay mare would cross his trail again.

IX

IN APRIL, when the new green grass was springing,
Uncle John took Cedar, along with four or five
young heifers, and placed them in a woods pasture on
the Davis farm, three miles up the Sheep Hill Road and
over the shoulder of the mountain. Bud accompanied him,
driving the cattle, with Tug's help, while the farmer led
Cedar on a halter. The colt had grown during the winter
and was a good-sized horse now. But he was lean and, as
Uncle John expressed it, "pithy." He needed filling out
and hardening. His winter coat, too, was shaggy and unkempt. Only to the eye of love could he have looked
handsome.

They reached the pasture at last, and Bud herded the
nervous heifers through the bars with a sigh of relief.
Uncle John took the halter off the colt's head and turned
him loose with a pat on the flank.

"Roughing it like this for a summer will do him good,"
he said. "He'll be a bit wild when we come back for him,
but that won't hurt. There's good sweet grass an' good

water, an plenty o' soft places to sleep up here. It'll make a horse of him."

The young cattle had strayed off among the clumps of pines at once, but Cedar stood by the bars, still looking after the man, the boy, and the dog until they passed out of sight over the hill.

Bud worked hard that spring. Every minute he could spare he helped Uncle John with the farming. Saturdays he was up at four-thirty and toiling steadily until dark. On Sundays after church he nearly always went off with Cal to one or another of their haunts in the woods. For this reason Bud missed the occasional trips that Uncle John took on Sabbath afternoons to visit the colt.

The clover and timothy ripened early that year and no sooner had school closed for the summer holidays than they began haying. For four weeks they worked like Trojans. Then at last came a hot July afternoon when the final load was under the shingles, and Uncle John, wiping the sweat from his sunburned face, grinned triumphantly at Bud.

"Well, son," he said, "now that the big job's done, we'll have a little breathin'-spell. What say we go up to the Davis lot tomorrow an' bring the colt down? It's time he had some schoolin'."

When the morning chores were done they hitched up old Betsy, put a halter and a pan of salt under the wagon seat, and started up the road.

The Davis pasture was a big, irregular tract of fifty

96

acres or more, covered with scattering young pines and thickets of birch. As the wagon stopped at the bars a bunch of half-wild heifers jumped away into the brush, then turned to watch the proceedings. With their wide, curious eyes and great ears they looked more like deer than cattle.

There was no sign of Cedar when they arrived. Uncle John took the pan of salt in one hand, and holding the halter in the other, behind him, he led the way along the inside of the rail fence. Occasionally he would stop and give a long, high-pitched whistle. At first there was no answering sound, and Bud's heart began to sink with misgiving. "He's gone," thought the boy. "He's been stolen!"

But just as the words were on the tip of his tongue there came a sudden thunder of hoofs, and out of the pines burst the colt, as beautiful as a flame. Bud caught his breath in wonder as the proud young horse raced down the slope toward them. His short summer coat glowed rich and ruddy, and the same warm tone shone in the full mane and long tail that streamed in the wind. Under his satiny skin the rippling shoulder muscles slipped as smoothly as a cat's. Wonderful, clean legs he had, and his chest had broadened, sweeping up into the base of his strong, arched neck.

All these impressions Bud caught in his first glance. Then Uncle John laid a hand on his arm, dropping the halter in his excitement. "Look there," he whispered. At

97

the words, Bud saw the colt drop from a gallop into the even, rocking gait of a natural pacer.

"I'd been hopin' fer that," said the farmer. "If it wasn't fer his color I'd take him fer Caribou, his dad. Come on, Cedar, boy, an' git your salt."

The colt came to a stop a dozen yards away. For a moment or two he was shy, sniffing at their extended hands, then leaping away with a toss of his red forelock. But in the end the delectable taste of salt won him over. Gently Uncle John buckled the halter strap about his throat, and after that they could stroke his sleek sides and velvet nose as much as they pleased.

Bud took his place in the back of the wagon, proudly holding the end of the halter rope, and they led Cedar back to the farm.

Uncle John had already prepared for the colt's return. From the back of the carriage house he had brought out an old high-wheeled road cart, and he had given Bud a busy half hour oiling up a set of stout, light harness. Cedar trembled a little when the girth was buckled around his smooth barrel, but under the farmer's steady hand and voice he quieted down.

Then the colt's education began in earnest. For an hour or more Uncle John walked behind him, up and down the fenced barnyard, guiding him with the reins, teaching him to start and stop at a word. At first Bud led him. Then came the moment when he stepped out alone with only the lines from the light bit in his mouth

THE COLT CAME TO A STOP A DOZEN YARDS AWAY

controlling his movements. Uncle John was gentle with him and amazingly patient, but always firm. And in spite of the colt's gay dash and spirit it soon became apparent that he was one of those rare horses that never have to be broken, in the harsher sense of the word.

On the second day the lesson was continued. After half an hour of it the gate of the barnyard was opened and still walking behind him, Uncle John guided Cedar out to the road. He was prepared to hold him even if he tried to bolt, but the colt made no effort to run. They went a few hundred yards up the highway and returned. Then the farmer backed him up to the road cart and very quietly let the shafts down on either side of him. There was an anxious half-minute while the colt quivered and snorted. The breeching was made fast and the traces fastened.

While Bud still held Cedar's head, Uncle John climbed into the seat, took a solid grip on the reins, and nodded for the boy to let go. At his cluck the colt started forward, felt the unaccustomed tug of the road cart, and reared up, terrified. Uncle John steadied him, brought him down on four feet again, and once more gave the signal to move. Hesitantly the sorrel took a stride and another, felt no ill effects, and went on, gaining in confidence.

Out on the open road Uncle John walked him until he was used to the feel of the vehicle behind him, then little by little urged him to a faster gait. When he brought him back, a quarter of an hour later, the colt was pacing as prettily as if he were free in the pasture.

Three more days of dancing up and down the highway, and Cedar was a real road horse—hardly perfect in his manners yet and a bit too sportively inclined, but a road horse nevertheless.

Uncle John was delighted. "This colt has got more common sense than most ten-year-old hosses," he told Bud. "There ain't a speck of meanness in him and never will be if I can help it. Why, I'd jest as lief drive him into Riverdale tomorrow. If I let him look at an automobile an' smell of it, he wouldn't wiggle an ear no matter how many of 'em should come roarin' by."

As a matter of fact it was only the next week that Cedar met his first car on the road and behaved with all the good sense for which his master gave him credit. After that it was but a short time before Bud was allowed to take him out on the back roads for exercise jogs.

Bursting with pride, the boy would climb to the seat of the road cart and settle himself on the cushion of old sacking which padded it. "Come on, now, Cedar," he would call and gather the reins. And at the word the big red colt would go out of the yard with his light, quick step, rocking into a pace the moment there was gravel under his feet. He was a tight-rein horse. Uncle John had taught him to respond with more and more speed to each added pressure on his velvet mouth. It was good to see his smooth-working legs flash in and out whenever Bud tightened his grip.

With them on their jaunts went Tug, and the bull terrier ran himself lean keeping up with the long, swift stride of the pacer.

Early in Cedar's training Uncle John had taken him to Cale Otis, whose blacksmith shop at the Four Corners was famous among horsemen all over the county. There the colt had been equipped with light road-shoes, weighted a trifle in front to give him needed reach. It was said that Otis, once he had seen a race horse step, never made a mistake in shoeing him. And certainly Cedar's marvelously smooth action on the road was a tribute to the burly smith's craft.

By the time frost came that autumn the word had spread up and down the township that John Mason had a pacing colt worth watching. Bud saw farmers look up from their work and point excitedly as he went by. Fair-time, in late September, found half the county milling around the midway and packing the grandstand at the races. Cedar was there. Solid-muscled now and proud of head, grown almost to his full strength, he snorted across the whitewashed rail and pawed the dust as the foam-flecked trotters sped past.

A short, gray-haired man stopped near the Mason carriage to watch the start of the 2.20 free-for-all. Uncle John nudged Bud and pointed with his thumb. "That's Ol' Billy Randall—prob'ly the best trainer in the state.

He's down here lookin' over young hosses fer his owners," explained the farmer.

On the track the big field of eight or nine racers came thudding down to the start. As they neared the line a high-strung mare broke and the close ranks were scattered. The petulant *clang-clang* of the starter's gong ran out, calling for a fresh try, and angry drivers sawed at their horses' mouths, wheeling them for the jog back to the post.

The gray-haired man shook his head disgustedly and turned toward Cedar. For a fleeting instant his eyes roved over the sorrel's body; then he strolled to the side of the wagon.

"Likely-lookin' colt, John," he remarked, touching his cap to Aunt Sarah. "Pacer, ain't he? Two-year-old?"

"Yes," said Uncle John, "he's one o' Caribou's colts. I'd be pleased fer you to try him, Billy."

"I don't hev to try him," said the other mildly, biting off an end of the grass stem he was chewing. "Ain't I got eyes? Tell you what. Why don't you turn him over to me fer a year?"

Uncle John shook his head. "Can't afford it, Billy," he laughed. The trainer shot a shrewd glance at him. "Want to sell?" he asked. "I know a man that might give a thousand fer a colt like that."

"No," said Uncle John. "I'm not sellin' this year." And the two men smiled at each other understandingly as Mr. Randall took his departure.

On the way home that night Bud spoke up from the rear seat. "Gosh, Uncle John," he said, "did Randall mean that about a thousand dollars?"

"I shouldn't be surprised," answered the farmer. "That's a lot o' money. More'n I make in a year, sometimes. Still, I think a lot o' this hoss. Guess I'll wait an' see what he looks like another season."

It was several weeks later on a chill evening in November that Bud was walking up the hill from the Corners, his school books in a strap over his shoulder. Already it was nearly dark, and he heard the clink of hoofs and the rattle of wheels coming down the frosty road before he could see what was approaching. When the rig was almost abreast of him he made out the form of a small dark horse, trotting fast, and a buggy with the top slouched over to the left. Led behind on a halter was another horse, a tall gray, so light in color that its pale sides loomed ghostly in the dusk. Bud stopped suddenly and watched the buggy until it was swallowed by the night. Harko Dan, the gypsy. Where, the boy wondered, was he hurrying—and why? As he slowly climbed the slope he tried to reassure himself. The gray was simply a trade, of course—some old nag to be fattened and sold at a profit. And yet, in spite of his own logic, Bud felt a vague uneasiness.

Snow fell early that fall. By Thanksgiving Day there was a six-inch blanket over the fields, and the firm-packed surface of the roads offered unusually fine sleighing.

There came a night of clear white moonlight, and when the evening chores were finished Uncle John told Bud to get on his mackinaw. "We're goin' to try Cedar in the cutter," he explained.

The big young horse had not been exercised in harness for three days. He reared and danced when Uncle John led him from his stall, and they kept the carriage house closed until he was hitched to the light sleigh. Then Bud rolled the big door back and made a leap for the seat as the cutter went past him. Like something shot from a catapult the red colt bounded out into the snow. As the cold air filled his nostrils he gave a mighty snort, then squared away to pace.

Down the long slope of Red Horse Hill they sped and up the next rise with Cedar's gait hardly slackening. His strong legs took the rhythm of the jingling bells and held it, mile after mile. Uncle John gave him his head till they reached the fork at Mad River Bridge, then swung him homeward. Bud never forgot the wild joy of that ride——the breathless rush of the wind and the excitement of their discovery of Cedar's speed. He was a snow-horse. Foaled in a December blizzard, snow was his natural element. He loved it. When they pulled up in front of the barn once more he was breathing deeply but with an amazing ease. And behind them were five hard miles of hill road that the colt had covered in something under twenty minutes.

X

"BUD," said Uncle John at breakfast one Saturday morning in December, "the road was a mite slippery yesterday, an' those shoes of Cedar's didn't hold. He ought to be sharpened up all 'round. I want you to take him down to the blacksmith shop this forenoon. Tell Cale Otis to use his judgment an' to pretend he's workin' on a 2.10 Grand Circuit hoss."

He said this last with a wink, but Bud refused to treat such a subject lightly. "Two-ten's going to be easy for Cedar," he said. "He'd do it this year if he had the chance. Didn't we time him in 2.26 on that flat stretch of the lower pike last week?"

"Humph!" Uncle John returned. "'Twa'n't a measured mile, an' goodness knows if that ol' silver turnip o' mine was right. We better not begin braggin' jest yet."

Bud hitched the lively young horse to the cutter and went tearing off down the road. At the foot of the hill, where the main highway crossed, he pulled up before the smithy. There was one horse there ahead of him, so he took Cedar out of the shafts, blanketed him, and tied him inside to wait.

In spite of the brisk cold of the winter morning, Bud

found it snug and warm beside the glowing forge. Cale Otis was making a heavy work shoe for one of Hunter's horses. In the corner on a bench sat Gideon, the French teamster, playing a mouth organ while the smith roared a mighty bass. Otis held the half-shaped shoe in a pair of long pincers gripped in his right hand, twisting and turning it in the fierce heat of the forge fire. With his huge left arm he pumped steadily at the bellows. When the shoe was white-hot he would place it across the nose of the anvil and with a few swift blows of the hammer beat it into the desired form. When it had cooled to a dull, dark red he would step to the horse's side, lift its hind foot to the lap of his leather apron, and try the shoe against the newly trimmed hoof. A smoke ascended, pungent and acrid. At last, when the iron crescent was properly shaped and the heavy calks set to suit him, the blacksmith pulled his tool-box over to the horse's side, picked up the hoof once more, and deftly nailed the shoe in place. As he finished filing the outside of the hoof, Otis wound up his bass solo with a flourish.

"Here ye be, Gid," he called cheerily. "Take yer hoss out o' this."

Then he turned to Bud. "So this young scamp of a pacer wants some winter shoes," he said. "Let's see how he stands." Critically he eyed the colt's feet, walking around him in a slow circle. "Hm," he said, at length, " 'twouldn't do a mite o' harm to build him up jest a shade on the outside o' that left front foot."

He ripped off the sorrel's shoes, trimmed his hoofs with a big two-handed knife, and set about fitting the summer plates with light, keen calks. While he worked he talked. "I s'pose John still says he won't race him this year," said the blacksmith. "Too bad, too bad. Why, this colt, if he had any proper handlin', could beat 2.30 before the winter's over."

Bud wanted to blurt out the story of the 2.26 mile but he recalled Uncle John's parting injunction and held his peace. All he said was, "I guess Cedar gets pretty good handling."

"We used to think a two-year-old was too young to race," Otis continued as he cunningly added a build-up strip to the side of the left front shoe. "Now look at 'em, though. The best ones beat 2.15 right along. Every year more youngsters get down in fast time. This feller's strong an' husky. 'Twouldn't hurt him a mite to train."

Just as the big blacksmith was nailing on the last of the four new shoes Cal Hunter came running across the road. He was beaming and breathless.

"Hi, there, Bud," he cried, "I've got the rest o' the mornin' off. What say we go some place? Can you get off?"

"Don't know," said Bud; "I'll find out. Want to go over to Caterwaul River and see if we can locate Grandpa Hartley's old house?"

"Sure," Cal answered. "I'll go home and get some grub together."

Uncle John not only told Bud he might make the trip, but let the boys take Cedar and the cutter. "It'll do him good to have the exercise," said the farmer. "Tie him fast, out o' the wind, and blanket him right, when you git there."

It was a fine, bright winter day and Cedar was anxious to show what he could do. His new calks kept him from slipping on the hard-packed highway, and even though Bud held down his speed, it still lacked an hour of noon when they reached the lonely back road on the slope of Hogback Mountain. They drove in on an abandoned wood track and hitched the horse in a sheltered place, then took the bundle of food Cal had brought, and struck off through the pines.

"If we keep bearin' down hill," said Cal, "we're bound to come to the river. An' once I get there, I know just about where the old farm used to be."

They went what seemed a long distance, climbing over fallen logs and skirting clumps of underbrush. It was hushed and windless on the snowy floor of the forest, but overhead they could see the tops of the big pines tossing and hear a muffled sound like surf beating on a distant shore.

Cal cast a keen eye aloft. "Jiminy!" said he. "I wonder if Paw ever cruised this lot. He likes to look at big timber, an' I bet he never saw a prettier stand o' pine than this. There's lots o' trees here that would cut a thousand feet o' clear lumber. Just the part we've come through, 'tween here an' the road, would make close to a million feet."

They came to a place where the hillside dropped away

more steeply, and Bud, in the lead, caught a glimpse of a curving white ribbon through the trees. "There she is," he called and went plowing down the slope at a run. In another minute they had reached the bank of the little river. It was only a dozen yards across at the point where they stood, and even in the grip of winter it ran so swiftly that in many places openings in the ice showed the brown water brawling over the rocks.

Cal chuckled. "Hear her carry on!" he said. "Does sound sort o' like a cat, don't she?"

They followed the winding bank downstream and came to an old tumbling stone wall with a brush-grown clearing beyond it. A moment later they found themselves in a half-obliterated wagon road, leading diagonally up the hill from the stream.

"This is it," Cal announced. "This path runs right up to the Hartley place." As they advanced a queer excitement filled Bud. At last he was going to see the farm that had been his mother's home. He walked ahead eagerly, watching each curve in the winding road. Then of a sudden he stopped and raised his hand in warning.

"Listen," he whispered. "Did you hear that? I was sure I heard a horse whinny." They stood still a moment, but the sound was not repeated.

As they started forward again, however, Cal touched Bud on the arm and pointed upward, over the clumps of pine and birch. A thin wisp of smoke curled past on

112

the wind. "Come on," said Cal. "Let's see who's there, anyway."

They came out in an old orchard and moved on cautiously to a place where the road passed through an opening in another stone wall.

Cal pointed ahead. "That's what's left o' the house," he said. Bud looked, and his heart sank in disappointment. Even though he knew the place had been burned years before, his imagination had somehow painted a stately and homelike ruin. Instead he saw a pitifully naked brick chimney rising out of a mass of blackened débris partly covered with snow.

Old, gnarled apple trees surrounded the site of the house. Behind and to the right a few charred timbers showed where the barn had stood. And still farther back, under a big maple, the boys saw a crazy lean-to shed which had apparently escaped the conflagration. There was no sound, no movement. The place seemed utterly dead. And yet a moment before Bud would have sworn there was some one there.

"Come on," said Cal, "I'm hungry. We can start our fire and git the bacon fryin' an' then look around. That smoke must have been from a train somewheres."

He led the way up through the desolate dooryard and past the big, bare lilac bush by what had once been the front steps. "Here," he said, skirting the hollow of the old cellar, "back in the lee of the chimney ought to be a good place. If you see any firewood bring it along."

113

Ten seconds later they halted by the blackened brick-work of the chimney and stared at each other. There at the foot of the masonry was a rude open fireplace from which a tiny curl of smoke issued. Snow had been thrown over the fire and trampled down in an effort to extinguish it. Close beside was a pile of dry wood, and in all directions were tracks—moccasin tracks.

"Who in thunder—" muttered Cal, stooping above one of the clearest impressions. "Say, look here, Bud! This foot's a lot smaller'n mine. Must be a boy made the tracks. But why was he so scared when he sighted us? An' where did he skip to?"

"Let's follow his trail and find out," said Bud. "Here's one line of tracks going off this way." They traced the footprints past the burned barn and onward for fifty yards. Then the trail joined another much-trampled path coming down diagonally from the far side of the clearing.

"This just leads to the well," said Cal. And sure enough, in a few more steps they came to some planks laid loosely over a low circle of bricks. Bud lifted one and saw water gleaming blackly far below. Beside the well-curb stood an ice-coated pail with a long rope attached to its handle.

The boys cast about vainly for some clew to the direction taken by the moccasin-shod stranger. There were tracks in plenty all about the old farmyard, but none seemed to lead away toward the woods.

"What do you s'pose is back in that lean-to?" Bud

speculated. "The path to the well seemed to come from up that way." His question was answered as soon as it was spoken. From the rickety out-building at that moment came an unmistakable sound—the long-drawn snort of a horse. Both boys jumped at the noise.

"Well, I'll be jiggered!" gasped Cal. "You *did* hear a hoss—no mistake."

Bud was already on his way toward the shed. "I'm going to have a look at him," he said. Together they approached the sagging door and paused with thudding hearts. Bud placed his eye to a crack and tried to peer in. "Can't see a thing," he whispered. "It's dark inside."

"All right," said Cal, "I'm going to open the door." He tried the wooden latch cautiously, and it gave with a creak under his hand. Little by little he pulled the door outward, until both he and Bud could see the whole interior of the shack. There was straw on the floor and a half-empty grain sack in one corner. Hitched to a beam at the farther side stood a tall gray horse, blanketed with old bagging.

"Say, boy, that's a real hoss!" exclaimed Cal. "A trotter, I bet yer. He's got a good head an' pretty legs."

Bud was thinking—trying to remember. Where had he seen that horse before? A pale gray, almost white— like a ghost— He had it! The horse that had been led behind the gypsy's buggy that night a month before!

"Listen, Cal," he said. "There's something queer about this. I don't like it. Let's get back to the road."

Cal looked at him in amazement. "What's the matter?" he asked. "Aren't we going to cook this grub that I've lugged for two miles?"

"Come on," urged Bud. "I'll carry the grub, and we'll eat it somewhere else. I don't want to leave Cedar a minute longer than I have to. I've just got a hunch that white horse has been *stolen!*"

They found a rutted wood road leading up the hill from the edge of the clearing. As they hurried along it Bud explained the reasons back of his suspicions. Cal was inclined to scoff at the idea. "Why, there ain't been a hoss-thief in this county since before I was born," he said. "That's all imagination. These gypsies go around swappin' hosses, an' o' course they cheat like sin in a trade, but that's as fur as they dare go. What I'd like to know is who built that fire an' why he was so quick to hide when we came in sight."

Their discussion of this mystery lasted all the way out to the Danford Pike, and it was still unsolved when they came in sight of the wood road where they had driven in. To Bud's great relief Cedar was still standing in the shelter of the pines. Under the seat of the sleigh they had brought a box of oats, and this was placed on a stump for the horse's noon meal. There was a ledge of rock near by, and against it the boys piled a pyramid of dry wood which they soon had blazing brightly. While the bacon sputtered in the pan and the water boiled for cocoa, Cal sliced a crisp loaf of his mother's home-made bread. In a few minutes they were munching bacon sandwiches.

"Say, Bud," announced Cal between mouthfuls, "I don't know about you, but I'm goin' back to that house sometime mighty soon an' find out what became o' the kid in moccasins. He was hid somewhere right there around the old house, as sure as you're a foot high. I know you won't want to bring Cedar over here again, but how about hikin' over? Christmas vacation begins next week. What do you say?"

"Sure," Bud agreed heartily. "I'd like to explore that place a bit myself. I'm not satisfied yet about the white horse. Cal, if there *was* a horse thief at work and we could help catch him—gee!"

"Huh!" laughed Cal. "You still thinkin' about that? You ain't even sure it's the same hoss you saw this gypsy feller leadin'. It was pitch dark, wasn't it? An' there's lots o' white an' gray hosses in New Hampshire."

Bud had no argument to offer, but he remained unconvinced. "All right," was all he said. "Wait and see."

They finished their meal and put out the fire. Cedar, impatient from standing in the cold, was more than willing to start for home. On the first level stretch he limbered up his legs and cut loose with a whirlwind burst of speed.

"Jupiter fishhooks!" cried Cal as he clung to the edge of the seat. "Bud, if this feller ain't entered in the Speedway Races this year it'll be a durn shame. He can trim any o' those nags, or I'm a wall-eyed shad!"

117

XI

CHRISTMAS vacation was anything but a season of loafing on Red Horse Hill. Outside of some coasting parties when the moon was full Bud and Cal saw little of each other during the two weeks.

Uncle John had given Bud the job of thinning out the birches in the upper pasture, and he spent his days swinging an ax. When the red dawn blazed in the east and warmed the grim, snowy tops of the hills with rose, he would go up the mountainside. Down again at noon for one of Aunt Sarah's famous dinners, then back to the birches until the fall of dusk. When he "got his hand in," as Uncle John put it, the boy was cutting and piling better than two cords of birch every day.

New Year's fell on Monday, and school was to begin the next day. On Saturday morning Uncle John told Bud while they were milking that he could have the day off. "Likely you an' Cal have got some sort of a trip you want to take," he said. "I wouldn't git off too far, though. It looked like a storm last night."

True to the farmer's prediction, the day broke gray and bleak. After breakfast Bud put on his sweater and a sheep-lined coat he had been given for Christmas, called his dog, and set out down the road. At Hunter's he found Cal just finishing his wheat cakes and sausage. He, too, had been given a holiday. Throughout the vacation he had been driving a team for his father, hauling wood to a brickyard near Riverdale.

"How about that hike we planned over Danford way?" suggested Bud. "It looks stormy, but we'll be back before it starts."

"Fine," said Cal. "That's just what I've been wantin' to do. Soon as I pack up some provisions in a knapsack we'll get off."

Bud laughed at the amount of food the towhead put in his pack. "You must expect company for dinner," he said.

"Boy, you'll be glad enough to have it when you've walked five miles," Cal replied with some heat. "An' then there's Tug—don't he eat as much as two grown men?"

An hour and a half of steady hiking brought them to the side of Hogback Mountain, overlooking the narrow valley of the Caterwaul. This time they had no difficulty in locating the wood road that led down to the old Hartley place.

"Go easy, now," Cal cautioned. "We were talkin' an' makin' plenty o' noise when we came up from the river that last trip. Let's see if we can't take 'em by surprise —real Injun stuff."

As they approached the edge of the clearing they left the path and stole through the woods, treading carefully and keeping a sharp watch ahead. Tug, who had often stalked woodchucks with his master, stayed close beside him, silent and alert.

An old stone wall stood at the edge of the woods, and crouching behind it, the boys were able to get a fair view of the burned house some three hundred yards away. Once more they saw smoke ascending, and after a moment something moved at the foot of the bare chimney.

Bud nudged Cal. "There he is!" he whispered. "How are we going to get across the field without his seeing us?"

"We'll have to stay hid the best we can behind those apple trees," said Cal. "Keep low an' follow me."

He crawled over the wall, and stooping almost double, started toward the nearest tree. Close behind him ran Bud and the white terrier. Just before they reached their goal Bud glanced toward the ruined house and saw a sudden movement. A whispered exclamation came from Cal. Standing in the shelter of a thick, gnarled trunk, he was staring at the chimney, a puzzled look on his face.

"Doggone!" he breathed as Bud joined him. "I never seen anything as quick as that. He jest looked up an' then ducked. Went out o' sight quicker'n you could say scat!"

"Are you sure he saw us?" asked Bud.

"Yep, he saw us all right," said Cal. "He dropped as if he'd been shot."

"There's no use in our hiding, then," Bud said. "We might just as well walk down there and hail him. Come on."

They crossed the clearing and came to the chimney, where the fire was still burning. Cal went on to look around the pit of the cellar, but Bud stopped, bending over something in the snow. It was a piece of stiff wire, three or four feet long, on which the carcass of a small animal had been spitted. The partly roasted flesh was still warm from the fire.

Bud picked up the hot wire in his mittened hand and beckoned to Cal. "Look," he said when the other boy had rejoined him, "here's what he was cooking for dinner. Must be a red squirrel, isn't it?"

"That or a chipmunk," said Cal. "Not much more'n a mouthful, whatever 'tis. Say—look at that dog! What's he up to?"

Tug had jumped down to the snowy floor of the cellar and was nosing eagerly at a board that filled the narrow space between the chimney base and the cellar wall.

"What is it, boy—rats?" asked Bud.

The terrier barked and started scratching at the board. "He's found something. Let's take a look," said his master.

They dropped into the hollow and hurried toward the dog. Behind him Bud heard Cal's excited whisper and

121

turned to see the other boy pointing at a moccasin track in the snow close to the wall. He nodded and jerked his mittened thumb toward the board. When the boys reached it Bud called Tug back out of the way, and together he and Cal gripped the edge. "All right, pull!" muttered Cal. The board gave so suddenly that they nearly fell backward in the snow. On the back of it they saw a staple with a piece of rope attached. And beyond, in the rear of the chimney foundation, was a yawning black hole.

Tug sprang forward with a growl, but Bud seized his collar, preventing him from rushing into the opening. For a moment the boys waited, not knowing just what to expect. Then Cal, in his deepest and roughest voice, shouted, "Better come out o' that!"

There was a noise of movement in the hole, and they saw a boy crawl forth. He was a thin little figure, not more than twelve years old, judging from his size, but his face was strangely old. And in his deep-set black eyes was a desperate fear that made Bud think, with a twinge, of an animal caught in a trap. As the boy stood erect they saw his clothes, and Cal drew in his breath in a whistle of amazement. The youngster had on loose trousers of some thin cottony material that had once been red. They were so tattered and stained that little of the original color remained. A tight jacket of faded black velvet came to his waist. There were remnants of gilt braid on the cuffs and down the breast of the garment. It failed to meet in front by inches, and an ancient cotton undershirt

122

filled the interval. Around his throat the boy wore a red handkerchief. His head was covered only by a touseled mat of hair.

"What do you want?" he whispered huskily. His lips were blue with cold, and his teeth chattered constantly.

"We came to look at the place," said Bud. "My folks used to live here. Why are you so scared to see anybody?"

The youngster stared back at him wildly, his mouth shut in a desperate line.

"Was that your dinner you was cookin'—that squirrel?" asked Cal.

The boy nodded slowly.

"Listen," Cal went on, gruffly, "is that all you've got to eat?"

"Yes, it's all!" cried the lad with a sudden fierceness. "An' if you take it—you——" He ripped out a string of oaths and drew a wicked-looking knife from his rear pocket.

"Hey! Go easy!" gasped Cal, taking a step backward. "You got me all wrong, kid. I was goin' to say we've got heaps o' grub, an' if you'll let us use your fireplace we'd like t' have you eat with us."

The boy looked at him open-mouthed as if he did not take in what had been said. Then as suddenly as he had drawn the knife he replaced it and burst into tears.

Bud took him by the arm. "Come on," said he, "let's get things cooking before that fire goes out."

They climbed out of the cellar, and while Bud replenished the blaze Cal started taking food out of the knapsack. The strange boy's eyes bulged at the sight of bread, bacon, and potatoes. And Bud, who knew something about hunger himself, pulled out his knife, cut a generous slice of bread, buttered it, and put it in the youngster's hand. He ate it like an animal, ravenously, and watched them all the while through narrowed eyes as if he feared that the food would be snatched from him.

"Gosh all hemlock," cried Cal, "you *did* have an appetite! Don't you have any home to go to for real grub?"

The boy shook his head as he stuffed the last of the bread into his mouth.

"You mean you hang around here all the time?" asked Bud in amazement.

The boy hesitated a moment. Then, "Yeah—I have to," he said. "I work for a guy. I have to watch things here for him."

Cal did not seem satisfied with this explanation and started to ask another question, but Bud caught his eye and silenced him. "Don't hurry him," Bud whispered to his chum when an opportunity offered. "He'll talk when he isn't so scared."

There was a heap of dry wood close by the fireplace, and the boys soon had water heating for cocoa, and bacon and potatoes sizzling cheerfully.

When the food was ready Bud filled up a tin plate and a cup for the half-starved boy and chuckled to see him go to work on them. Little by little as the lad's hunger was abated they brought him into their conversation. And sure enough, under the friendly warmth of their treatment he began at last to talk.

His name, he said vaguely, was Yance. That was all. Just Yance. He used to live in Leather City, a settlement of half-breed Indians and gypsies on the other side of Hogback. Bud and Cal had heard of it. A squalid little place where no self-respecting person ever went if he could help it. The inhabitants wove wicker baskets and occasionally went through the neighboring towns, selling them.

Yance's father was drunk nearly all the time and made life so miserable for the boy that he had run away with a gypsy horse-trader to whom he referred as Danny. Bud and Cal exchanged a glance at the mention of the name. For a long time—three or four months, he thought—Yance had traveled around with the roving trader. Then they had come back here for the winter and Danny had made this old farm his "hang-out."

"He brings hosses here," the boy said. "Then when he goes off again I stay here an' take care of 'em. I sleep with 'em in the stable."

"That gray road hoss," said Cal. "Is he still here?"

The boy shook his head. "Danny took him away five or six nights ago," he answered.

" 'Round Christmas day?" asked Bud.

Yance looked blank. "I ain't kept track," he said. "Is it past Christmas?"

125

"You mean to say that skunk left you here without anything to eat?" Cal put in.

"He gave me some corn meal an' a little piece o' pork, an' he said he'd be back in two days," said Yance. "He ain't been back."

"You haven't any gun. How'd you ever get that squirrel you were roasting?" asked Bud.

"Stuck some corn meal out there on a chip an' waited for somethin' to come after it," Yance replied. "Then I kilt him with a pole."

The two older boys were silent while they finished their dinner—both, perhaps, thinking the same thoughts. Bud was the first to put his in words.

"This is no kind of a place for *anybody* to live," he said, setting down his empty plate. "Look—it's starting in to snow now." From the ominous gray sky the first big feathery flakes were zigzagging down. "You come on home with us, Yance," Bud finished.

"That's it," said Cal. "We'll find a good warm place for you to sleep in my barn, an' I'll sneak grub out to you. Come along."

"No!" cried the boy with something like terror in his voice. "If Danny came back an' I was gone he'd kill me!"

"Shucks—he couldn't find you," Cal laughed.

"Find me? You don't know Danny," said Yance. "No, I got to stay here."

For several minutes the two boys remonstrated with him, but all their arguments proved futile.

126

Finally Bud started unbuttoning his sheep-lined coat. "All right," he said, "here's this old sweater of mine. It's got a couple of holes in it, but it'll help keep you warm. You can put it on right over that gypsy jacket."

Cal was bending over the knapsack. "Here's four rolls an' half a loaf o' bread," he said. "An' quite a lot o' bacon, an' 'most half a peck o' spuds, an' some butter an' salt an' cocoa. Bud told me I was bringin' too much, an' I thought so, too, before I was through luggin' it. But now I ain't sorry. What's here ought to keep you from starvin' for a little spell anyhow."

The gypsy boy stood there in awkward silence. He did not seem to know how to thank them, and Bud hastened to his rescue. "You'll have to find a good snug place to keep this food so the snow won't spoil it," he said. "Want to carry it up to the lean-to?"

"No," said Yance. "I want it down here near the fire. That place down under the chimney where I was hidin' is fine an' dry."

He led the way down into the cellar while Bud and Cal followed, carrying the provisions. The hole in the brick foundation was about three feet high by two in width so that they had to crawl in on hands and knees. To their amazement there was room for all of them to stand erect when they got inside. A dim light entered from the aperture and after a few seconds their eyes became accustomed to the semi-darkness.

"Well, I'll be—" muttered Cal. "This place was *built*

fer a hide-out, sure enough. Look—a shelf an' everything.
We can clear out some o' this rubbish an' pile the grub
up here."

Bud was already fumbling in the litter on the shelf.
There was a sheaf of old papers tied with a string, and

in a corner, lying on its side, a small earthenware pot.
Lifting the pot, Bud's exploring hand touched something
under it that felt like a coin. He seized it and held it to
the light. It was an old silver half-dollar.

"Yeah," said Yance. "Danny found a lot of 'em in
that crock—more'n a hundred, I guess."

Cal gave a long whistle, but Bud said nothing. With
fingers that trembled a little with excitement he was

pulling one of the documents from the string-tied bundle. The other two boys stooped beside him as he knelt down, holding the paper close to the entrance. It was folded into a long, narrow, legal-looking shape and yellowed with age. Across the top, in faded blue ink, were written the words:

Last Will and Testament of
Silas Hartley

XII

BUD MARTIN felt a queer chokiness in his throat as he looked at the private papers of the grandfather he had never seen. The will was written entirely in longhand—the painfully neat but shaky handwriting of an old man—and the boys had difficulty in making some of it out.

First there was a lengthy preamble couched in legal phraseology. Then came a number of minor bequests. Finally they found the words:

". . . To my beloved daughter Jane Hartley Martin, wife of Thomas Martin, or to her issue in event of her death, I do give and bequeath my farm, situate between the Danford Road and the east bank of Caterwaul River in the town of Danford, together with all buildings and improvements thereon and all live stock, farming implements, house furnishings, produce, and standing timber."

The paper was signed with Silas Hartley's own name and those of two witnesses, Joshua Hayes and Raymond Carter. It was dated June 9, 1902, which, as nearly as

Bud could figure, was about a year before his grandfather's death.

"Jiminy Christmas!" cried Cal as Bud folded the will once more. "'Cordin' to that the whole durn place belongs to you, don't it? The timber on it must be worth twenty thousand dollars. Gosh, Bud, think of it!"

Bud tied the bundle of papers together with stumbling fingers. "That's what it seems to say," he answered. "But in law it may not mean a thing. I'll take these things along home and show 'em to Uncle John."

They crawled out of the hiding-place and climbed from the cellar to the level of the ground. Cal picked up his empty knapsack, and Bud whistled for Tug, who had been exploring the premises. He had a special whistle— two short, sharp notes and a long trill—that the terrier knew, and he came racing at the sound.

Little Yance had stood watching these preparations for departure in silence. Now he took an impulsive step forward. "Listen," he stammered. "I—I ain't never goin' to ferget this. If I can do somethin' for you fellers I will. I have to keep hid mostly, but if you come back, jes' whistle like you done for the dog, an' I'll know it's you."

"Sure, we'll come back," said Cal. "Just you keep a stiff upper lip, boy. We'll bring you some more grub an' see if we can't find a way to git you out o' this."

They said good-by and set out toward the woods. In a moment or two the stark black chimney and the little figure standing beside it had faded from sight in the thickly falling snow.

In spite of the storm the boys made good time on the return trip. The excitement of their discovery hastened their steps, and it was still daylight when Bud and his dog came plowing through the white blanket that lay deep in front of the doorstone on Red Horse Hill. The boy brushed off his snowy boots in the shed and looked into the kitchen. Aunt Sarah was bustling about, getting supper.

"See what I found in the cellar of the old Hartley place," Bud cried as he entered. "Where's Uncle John?"

"In the barn," she answered, adjusting her spectacles to read the paper that the boy thrust under her nose. Bud dashed out and a moment later returned with Mr. Mason in his wake.

"Land's sakes alive, John!" Aunt Sarah exclaimed. "Look here. If he hasn't found Silas Hartley's will! Why, the boy's rich!"

Uncle John refused to be stampeded. He read the document through twice and took it to the window for a thorough examination. Only then did he give vent to a low, thoughtful whistle. "Where'd you come across this, Bud?" he asked.

Bud described the hidden closet built into the brickwork of the chimney foundation. For the time being he decided to say nothing about the gypsy boy. Yance was his secret and Cal's.

As he finished the farmer nodded. "That's fine," he said. "Now don't git to countin' on this too heavy, Bud. You might be powerful disappointed. The will seems to be genuine an' all. But there's a lot o' possible complications. Property don't jest drop in people's laps. Tomorrow I'll have a talk with Sheriff Jim Gardner."

Sheriff Gardner was an old friend of Mr. Mason's. During the week his duties kept him at Merriton, the county seat, thirty miles away, but on Sundays he was usually to be found at home. After church the following day Uncle John hitched up old Betsy and with Bud in the sleigh drove down to the Gardner farm on the Mad River road.

The sheriff was reading his paper in the front parlor and came out to the porch to greet them as they blanketed the mare. He was a huge, jolly man with a deep, booming voice. When Bud had been introduced he ushered them into the comfortable parlor and gave them chairs. For a few minutes the two men talked of weather, politics, and friends, while Bud sat fascinated, watching the sheriff's great drooping mustaches and the massive gold chain across his stomach that jingled when he laughed.

Finally Uncle John came to the point of his visit. "I've brought the boy because this concerns him, Jim," he said. "You remember the old Hartley place, back in the woods near the Danford road? Well, Bud, here, is a relation of old Silas Hartley—his daughter Jenny's child. Yesterday Bud was over there lookin' at the ruins o' the house, an' he come across some papers. This was one of 'em."

He handed Sheriff Gardner the will and asked Bud to tell how and where he had found it. The boy went over his story once more, and the sheriff put on his glasses to read the document.

"Sweet Aunt Huldy!" roared the big man as he finished his perusal. "That's a great one! That farm is up for sheriff's sale right now. The state's been tryin' to locate the heirs, an' the taxes have piled up for years."

He turned and stared at Bud from under his bushy eyebrows. "Yes," he said, "I think I can see a family resemblance. Are you Jane Hartley's only child, Buddy?"

Bud nodded. In a few words he told the family's history as far as he knew it.

"Hm!" mused the sheriff. "John, you'll have to have this will probated, of course. I'll try an' get quick action on it from Judge Coburn. Then there's the matter o' provin' the boy's identity. There's probably some records down to Boston that we can get. One reason we'll have to work fast is that the sale o' the property is scheduled fer some time in February. Let me see—" he thumbed a pocket notebook for a moment. "Here 'tis—February 25. If you can prove title to the place an' pay the back taxes —$920—before then, o' course the auction won't be held. I happen to know the Northeastern Lumber Company wants that fine timber, an' they're aimin' to buy it in cheap. They've got the rest o' the bidders scared off."

"Is that right? Sam Felton's company, eh?" said Uncle John. "Well, that's just another reason why I want to see Bud get his property."

For a few more minutes the two men discussed various legal angles of the subject, and then Uncle John and Bud took their departure. As old Betsy toiled up the hill through the new snow the farmer grinned down at Bud. "Looks as if you'd soon be real well-to-do," he said. "Only one thing worries me, an' that's the fact that Sam Felton wants the property. I've had dealin's with him once or twice, an' there was always trouble. Crooked as a ram's horn, that feller. We'll jest have to watch him every minute."

Bud was thoughtful. "Mr. Gardner told us we'd have to raise $920 for the back taxes," he said. "That's a lot of money."

"Not compared to the value o' the farm an' that handsome stand o' pine," said Uncle John. "I can borrow that easy enough from the bank when the time comes."

Uncle John lost no time in setting the machinery in motion for establishing Bud's kinship to Silas Hartley. As nearly as the boy could remember the dates, addresses, and other details in connection with his mother's marriage and his own birth he gave them to Mr. Mason, and the farmer wrote two letters that night. One was sent to the Bureau of Vital Statistics in Boston, and the other to the Board of Education.

"If these don't raise the information we want we'll

go down there ourselves an' git it," said Uncle John.

It was not until more than a week later that he stopped at the bank and mentioned the matter of the loan. That night he came home angry and puzzled. Aunt Sarah had the supper ready and Bud had finished the chores when Uncle John drove into the yard. He unharnessed Betsy and came in to take his chair at the head of the table.

There were wrinkles in his usually calm brow as he served the stew. "I was pretty sure we'd hear from Sam Felton before this thing was settled," he said, "but it's come a lot quicker'n I expected."

"Why—whatever's the trouble, John?" asked Aunt Sarah with concern.

"I told the cashier at the Riverdale Trust that I wanted to borrow a thousand dollars," he answered. "He was friendly as could be and said he guessed that would be easy. Then as a matter o' form he asked me what it was for, an' I told him. He went back into the rear office to git the president's word on it and stayed ten or fifteen minutes. When he come out I thought he looked kind o' sober. 'Sorry, John,' he says, 'we can't make you a loan fer that partic'lar purpose.' I asked why not, an' all he'd say was it was against the policy o' the bank."

"Was Felton in there?" asked Aunt Sarah.

"No—leastways I didn't see him," Uncle John replied. "But Sam's the chairman o' the board o' directors, an' his company's probably the biggest depositor in the bank."

"And they had the nerve to turn you down when you've banked with them fer thirty years?" asked Aunt Sarah indignantly. "Well, I hope you jest drew out your account an' took it over to the National Bank."

"No," said Uncle John. "I thought about that, but my account ain't worth much in itself, an' the Northeastern Lumber Company has some influence at the National, too."

Aunt Sarah had a number of things to say about banks in general and those in Riverdale in particular. But Bud and Uncle John ate their supper in gloomy silence. At the conclusion of the meal they helped Mrs. Mason clear the table, and then, while Bud spread out his school books, Uncle John sat down to read the paper. It was some minutes later that the farmer looked up and met Bud's glance.

"Guess there's one way we can raise that money if everything else falls through," he said. His eyes dropped before the boy's searching gaze and he shifted uneasily in his chair. "That offer that Billy Randall made is probably still good."

"Billy Randall? Who—the horse trainer?" asked Bud. "You—you don't mean you'd sell Cedar! Oh, gosh, Uncle John, you couldn't do that! Why, I'd rather see the farm go any day! If you talk like that I'll wish I'd never found the old will."

The farmer shook his head. "I'd hate to part with him, too," he said. "But it's a matter o' sound business. That farm an' the timber on it is worth a reg'lar fortune. I can't see you cheated out of all that jest fer a sentimental reason. Still, we don't have to think about it fer a few weeks yet."

Bud went back to his lessons, but his mind wandered. It troubled him that Uncle John should even have suggested such a thing as parting with the red pacer. No, it was unthinkable. There must be some other way. He went to bed still racking his brain for a solution to the problem.

It was on Main Street in Riverdale the next day that an idea came to him. He had gone downtown during the noon hour to buy a new egg-beater needed by Aunt Sarah. On the way back he passed a billboard between two stores and stopped, staring up at the poster he saw there. It was the headline that had caught his eye—a headline in letters two feet high—"$1,000!"

Even before Bud had finished reading the words he knew what he was going to do. Cedar must be in that race! The boy could hardly wait for school to be out that afternoon, and the barge had never seemed so slow as it toiled up the hills.

Bud hurried home and rushed out to the barn where Uncle John was at work. In a few breathless sentences he poured out his news. "And you know Cedar can win!" he finished. "You'll enter him, won't you, Uncle John?"

The farmer leaned on his hay fork and chewed a straw of timothy. As he looked at Bud his eyes twinkled.

"You're jest a mite previous, aren't you, son?" he asked. "Cedar looks like a good colt—to us, anyhow. But don't go an' spend that thousand dollars yet awhile. Remember this—there's more good snow racers in New

$1000 to the WINNER
FREE-FOR-ALL MEETING
FOR THE
SNOW-RACING
CHAMPIONSHIP
OF NEW ENGLAND

RIVERDALE SPEEDWAY
FEB - 21-22

England than you an' I have ever seen. They'll come from all over, I jedge."

"All right," said Bud stoutly. "I've watched the best ones in Riverdale, and I'll bet on Cedar against that bunch."

"How 'bout this blue roan Chocorua mare o' Felton's?" suggested Uncle John.

"Gee," muttered Bud, "I'd forgotten her, but anyway Cedar could give her a race."

"Well," said Uncle John, "we'll think it over, an' it won't hurt to git the colt in trainin'. I might drive him, though I wouldn't have much expectation of walkin' off with the purse. Better git on your overalls, Bud. There's two or three little things like milkin' an' such to be done right now."

XIII

"BUD, could you get together a bag o' food by to-night—some apples an' potatoes an' maybe some bread or crackers?"

It was Cal Hunter talking as the two boys waited together for the school barge the next morning. "You know," he went on, "this boy Yance must be kind o' hungry again. I meant to git over there earlier, but there hasn't been a chance."

"I can get the potatoes and apples—yes, and crackers, too," said Bud. "But how do you think we're going to make it over there and back tonight?"

"Easy," Cal replied. "We'll take our sleds—it's good coastin'—an' Leo is drivin' over to Danford to see his girl. We'll hitch behind his cutter. Comin' back I guess we can make out to walk. You be down here at seven o'clock an' I'll tell Leo so he'll wait fer us."

After supper that evening Bud took his sled and told Aunt Sarah he was going down to Cal's. On the way out he picked up the bag of food which he had cached in a dark corner of the shed, and a quarter of an hour later he and Cal were tying their sleds to the rear braces of Leo's cutter. The young Frenchman had a tough little Canadian nag of which he was inordinately proud.

"Thees hoss," he explained, "she's Canada one. She'll work lak son-of-a-gun all day an' trot lak wan race hoss all night."

How much truth there was in this statement the boys soon discovered, for the little horse, taken off the wood hauling only two hours earlier, started off like a steam engine. All the way to the foot of Hogback Mountain Bud and Cal clung to the swaying sleds and shielded their faces from the clods of snow that came flying back from the hoofs of Leo's steed. In less than half an hour they reached the entrance of the wood road that led down to the Hartley farm.

There was a young moon that shed a faint light over the shadowy woodland. The boys unhitched their sleds and said good night to Leo, who would not be coming back till morning.

It was so still in the woods that the crunch of their shoes in the snow echoed sharply among the trees. They spoke in whispers. Before they had gone fifty yards Cal motioned to Bud and showed him some sleigh tracks. "Fresh since the last snow," he said. "This Danny feller must've come in here right lately. I can't tell whether he's here now. There's two or three sets o' tracks headin' both ways."

They went on cautiously to the edge of the clearing

and Bud tried his whistle, low and quiet. The second time he whistled a black shape became visible near the lean-to stable. "Look out," breathed Bud. "Stay where you are. That may not be Yance."

But as the figure drew nearer and answered with a crude imitation of the same whistled notes they were reassured. The gypsy boy came toward them warily, stopping now and then to peer at them through the gloom.

"It's all right, Yance," called Bud. "We've brought you some grub." At the words Yance hurried forward, and they met in the middle of the clearing near one of the old apple trees.

"Gee," said the gypsy lad, looking at the bag of food, "you sure brung a lot. Only I don't need it now. Danny's goin' away somewheres pretty quick, an' I've got to go back to Leather City. My ol' man's comin' to git me— mebbe tonight."

Bud stared at him in surprise. "Do you want to go?" he asked.

"Don't keer," the boy replied indifferently. "I been half froze here, an' lonesome, too."

"Yes," Cal started to expostulate, "but Leather City—"

His words were cut short by a sudden shout from the direction of the wood road. "Hey!" It was a man's voice, deep and menacing. Spinning to face the sound, the boys saw two men coming toward them across the clearing. One was big and slouching, the other slighter in build.

"Run!" gasped Yance. "It's them, now!"

Cal thrust out a stubborn jaw. "I ain't afraid," he said.

"We'll stay, Yance, and see they don't hurt you," Bud put in.

The gypsy boy seemed to be in an agony of fear. "Go! Go!" he whispered imploringly. "Danny's bad. He's got a knife."

Cal looked at Bud, and the latter shook his head. They stood their ground while the men drew near. Bud thought he recognized Harko Dan in the smaller of the two. When the man spoke he was sure of it.

"Well," came the remembered voice, "what are *you* lookin' for?"

The man leaned forward, peering closely into their faces in the moonlight while he kept his own visage in shadow.

"We're not looking for anything," Bud answered. "This boy's a friend of ours, an' we brought him something to eat."

Harko Dan swore venomously under his breath. "I'll see he gits enough to eat without no help," he said. "Do you know what happens to folks that come meddlin' in private business? Lucky thing fer you I ain't got a gun with me. I'd fill your breeches full o' birdshot!"

The big man took a stride forward and laid hold of Yance's wrist. "Don't try sneakin' off again, you rat!" he rumbled, in a voice that was thick with liquor. "You're a-comin' on home with me."

"Now clear out, the two of ye," snarled Harko **Dan** with an oath. "An' make it quick, 'fore I decide to cut your hearts out!"

He thrust his right hand under his coat and as he drew it out the moon flashed on bright steel. Both the boys started backward involuntarily. Bud touched Cal's sleeve. "Come on," he whispered.

"Well, so long, Yance," said Cal, and picked up his sled rope. Together he and Bud turned and set out on the back trail.

The gypsy horse-trader's voice came to them as they reached the edge of the woods. "Don't ye ever come in here again," he shouted. "I've got a special place to hide the carcasses o' kids like you."

Cal couldn't resist answering. "Aw, go jump in the river!" he called, then plunged into the dark tunnel of the wood road. Side by side the boys ran until their breath was gone, and stopped at last when they reached the Danford road.

"Golly," panted Cal, "whether that guy meant it or not I'm glad to git out o' his company. I don't like knives an' such foreign weapons."

"Neither do I," Bud agreed fervently. "And what's more, I've got a hunch he wasn't fooling. I tell you that gypsy's dangerous. I've watched him in the light when I could see his face."

They hiked the four miles home along the snowy roads, still pulling their sleds after them. Occasionally they would come to a down grade where it was possible to save time by coasting. For the most part they said little. The experience of the evening was still too vivid in their minds. But every once in a while one of them would express his thoughts.

"Gee," said Cal, "if you git to own that property next month, won't we tell Harko Dan where to get off! I'd like to be 'pointed a deputy sheriff so I could take a shot at him myself."

Bud too chuckled at the idea. Then he grew sober. "What I hate to think of is poor Yance going back to Leather City with that big bully of a father of his," he said.

"You're right," Cal answered. "We've got to git him out o' that some way or other. He'd be a pretty good kid if he had enough to eat an' a decent place to live. Say— speakin' o' things to eat, I wonder if Yance'll git any o' that bag o' grub we left down there."

Uncle John was still sitting beside the dining-room lamp when Bud reached home at ten o'clock. To the boy's relief he asked no questions beyond a general one regarding the weather. "I hope it'll stay clear an' cold for a while so this sleighin' will last," the farmer said. "I want to give Cedar a work-out every day from now on."

He rose to poke the fire and put on a huge chunk of maple to last through the night. "I drove him down to the Eagle Hotel an' had a talk with Billy Randall to-day," Uncle John went on. "He took the reins over him fer a spell an' the colt sure did his prettiest. Billy ain't one to talk much, but he thinks we've got a real hoss an' maybe even a chance fer second money down at River-dale. This Chocorua mare is sure to win, he says, unless they bring in somethin' extra good from outside."

Uncle John hesitated a moment, then went on slowly, a note of excitement in his voice. "If we handle the colt right," he said, "Billy thinks he'll step a mile in 2.10 before this winter's over."

Bud's eyes shone. "I knew it," he nodded. "Didn't I say he would?"

The following Saturday was overcast, with spits of snow, and the day was spent in sawing and splitting wood for the next year's fires. But Sunday dawned clear, and in the afternoon Uncle John and Bud drove Cedar to the level reaches of the valley road for his work-out.

There was a mile of almost straight highway, with little traffic and an excellent surface. When they reached the head of the stretch Bud started to climb out, but Uncle John told him to sit still. "Trainin' a colt, accordin' to Bill Randall, it's a good thing to have a load in the cutter. He gits used to pullin' the weight, an' when he starts to race the difference is all in his favor. Here, you hold the watch. It's a measured mile from the next fence corner down to Joe Parker's gate. I'll take him down at a four-minute clip an' come back a little faster. Then we'll breathe him a spell an' hit the third mile around 2.30."

The colt was well warmed up from his jog down the

147

hill and paced easily, knowing from experience what was expected of him. The old silver timepiece Bud held was not a stop-watch, but he could time their progress with fair accuracy.

"Four minutes and five seconds," the boy announced as they passed the Parker driveway.

Uncle John turned the big sorrel and headed him back without stopping. "Three-thirty fer this one," he remarked, gathering the reins a little closer. Cedar lengthened his stride and rocked along at a gait that gave Bud a thrill of pleasure, but the colt was still breathing easily when they got back to the head of the stretch.

"You hit that exactly right—three and a half minutes, even," Bud reported. They blanketed the young horse and walked him slowly up and down for a quarter of an hour.

"There," said Uncle John, "he ought to be about right now to step out. I'll take him up the road a ways an' git a flyin' start."

Turning a few hundred yards up the road, they picked up gradually, and as they passed the fence corner the farmer leaned forward, taking a tighter hold. Cedar thrust his neck out, and his tail came streaming back almost into their faces. Bud gripped the watch and his eyes moved back and forth from its broad dial to the flying colt. He had never seen him pace so fast. His reach was longer and his drive more powerful than in the summer.

148

The distant barn of the Parker place seemed to rush toward them. Bud saw the second-hand of the watch make its circuit once, twice, and start downward for the third time.

"Here we be!" called Uncle John through the furious beat of the sleighbells. Bud marked the second with his thumb-nail and leaned forward, staring hard at the watch.

"What did you make it?" asked the farmer when he had pulled the sorrel down to a walk once more.

"Jiminy Christmas!" Bud sputtered. "I must have seen it wrong. No, I didn't! It was just two seconds before the minute when we passed the start. And when you hollered it was nine seconds after the minute. But gosh, that's only two-eleven!"

Uncle John beamed and nodded. "Mebbe I yelled a bit soon," he said. "Call it two seconds more. That's two-thirteen. I guess that's about right. The way he went at it, I knew we were travelin'."

The colt was still fresh and eager as they jogged him back up the road, but Uncle John quieted him with his voice, crooning a constant "So-o-o, boy, easy there— steady now." It was about midway of the mile stretch that they met a nondescript cutter drawn by a quick-stepping little bay mare. Slouched back in the seat and holding the reins in one careless hand sat a man whose dark face was shadowed by a low-brimmed felt hat. Bud recalled that the rig had been close behind them when they had started down for the last mile. Then he looked again at the little mare and gave a jump. The man in the sleigh was the gypsy horse-trader, Harko Dan. He did not recognize Bud, but the boy thought he caught the flicker of a sardonic grin around the hard-bitten mouth as the two cutters passed.

"Who was that feller?" asked Uncle John. "Seems to me I've seen him before."

"Yes," said Bud, "he's the gypsy that came in the barn looking for a job back last spring."

"That's who 'tis, sure enough!" the farmer nodded. "I didn't like him then, an' my opinion of him ain't improved a mite."

Bud squirmed a little under the buffalo robe as he thought of the gypsy's keen black eyes and the way they had studied the handsome sorrel colt. But he made no reply.

They drove up Red Horse Hill and into the barn. Cedar was rubbed down carefully and shut into his roomy box-stall. Then they donned their overalls and set about the evening chores.

At the supper table that night Uncle John was more expansive regarding the colt and his chances in the coming race than Bud had ever seen him before. "Two-thirteen on that road," he told Aunt Sarah, "is mighty close to 2.10 on the speedway. An' then, too, he wasn't pushed. In a race, against real competition, he might even beat that time. The only thing we can't tell yet is whether he'll git nervous an' skittish with other hosses on the track. But I'll bank on him. He's got too much o' Betsy's good sense to act foolish."

Bud went to bed early in order to be ready for school next day. When he opened the window he looked at the night. It was cold and clear, but there was no moon. The stars seemed to snap and sparkle in the frosty ether. Bud yawned, climbed under the thick pile of covers, and in a moment was so sound asleep that you would have said nothing short of an earthquake could waken him.

But something did. It was a long time later, in the small hours after midnight, that Tug began to bark. The terrier often woke and gave tongue in the night. A team passing late, a fox prowling past the hen-house—any one of a dozen things might cause a brief outburst of sound from the restless dog. This was different. The barking kept on and grew louder, fiercer, more breathless.

Bud turned over in his sleep, sighing. Then as the terrier's din continued the boy suddenly opened his eyes, wide awake. He raised himself on one elbow, listening. There was a creak of floor boards from below. Like a flash Bud slipped out of bed and began throwing on his clothes. A moment later he was hurrying down the stairs. There was a lamp burning in the kitchen, and the shed door stood ajar.

Bud rushed out through the carriage house, following the faint beam of lantern-light that shone from the barn. There he came on Uncle John and Tug. The farmer stood at the far end of the floor by Cedar's box stall holding the lantern high over his head. From the look on his face Bud knew that something was wrong.

"What's the matter?" he started to ask, and then he saw. The gate of the stall was open and the colt was gone.

XIV

FOR a moment Uncle John was like a man in a daze.
Then he started frantically toward the tie-up and
the other horse stalls.

"Maybe he just got out. Maybe he's here in the barn!"
he said. The cattle were awake and on their feet, rest-
lessly shaking the stanchions. Old Betsy and Prince could
be heard moving in their stalls. But the young pacer was
nowhere to be found.

Bud went to the rear door of the barn and felt of its
fastenings. They were undone. The door rolled back at
his push. There were traces of snow on the sill and tracks
in the lane outside. At the boy's call Uncle John came
hurrying with the lantern. He looked at the tracks—a
man's boot-tracks and the dainty prints of the pacer's
feet.

"Yes," he said. "He's been stolen, right enough. Here,
take the lantern an' follow 'em while I git some shoes
on." He shivered as he spoke, for he had come out in
nothing more than a pair of cloth slippers and his trousers
pulled up over his nightshirt. Though not warmly

dressed, Bud at least had on his shoes. He seized the lantern eagerly and followed Tug out into the wide darkness.

The double trail led straight down the lane to the left. Forty yards from .the barn it passed through the open bars of the gate and thence into the road. There was a trampled space at the edge of the deep-worn sleigh ruts —a crisscross jumble of tracks. Which way had the horse thief gone? Bud cast back and forth desperately, but there was no means of telling. Tug whimpered and sniffed, then looked up, as baffled as his master.

The boy went back to the barn and met Uncle John returning fully dressed. "Here, you go in an' git on some warm clothes," said the farmer. "I'll see if I can find any signs out there."

Three minutes later Bud was back in mackinaw and cap. Uncle John was stooping over the roadside tracks. "Looks to me as if they'd drove a cutter up here to the edge o' the road. When they led Cedar out the lane they had some trouble gittin' him hitched behind. That's what all this tramplin' is from. But whether they went on over the hill or back toward the forks is more'n I can tell."

He rose and stood a moment, considering. "There's only one thing to be done now, an' that's rouse out the neighbors. The nearest telephone's down to Myron Hunter's. You run down there an' git Myron to call up the sheriff an' the chief o' police in Riverdale. I'll go up the road to the next two or three farms an' we'll have a crowd out after 'em by daylight."

Bud left Tug to guard Aunt Sarah and set out at a run down the snowy slope. As he ran his mind was busy with the catastrophe that had come to them and its possible consequences. Cedar gone! He had not realized how strongly they had all been counting on the young horse in the coming race. Persistently through his thoughts flashed the dark, evil face of Harko Dan. To Bud, at least, it was certain that the gypsy had stolen the colt.

Winded and panting, he reached the Hunter farm at last. It stood dark in the starlight—all its occupants sound asleep. Bud ran up the steps of the house and pounded on the door. In a moment Myron Hunter thrust his head out of an upstairs window and Bud gasped out his news. The farmer was wide awake in an instant. "I'll be down right off," he said and disappeared. There were sounds of activity within and soon the door opened.

Inside, Bud told the tousle-headed Cal and his father what had happened. For what seemed a weary while Myron Hunter stood at the farm-line telephone and rang and rang. At last he got the police station in Riverdale. In a few words he gave the facts. "No," he said in answer to a question. "No way to tell. Looks like they was leadin' him behind a sleigh. We'll git the neighbors out, but the thieves are probably a good four or five miles off by now. Yes—three-year-old sorrel colt. Pacer. That's the hoss. You bet he's a good one! Will you call the sheriff an' the other towns around? Right!"

He hung up. "They'll notify the police to watch all the main roads," he said briefly. "Now, Cal, you git dressed too, an' we'll spread the alarm."

In an incredibly short time Cal was ready. "Come on," he said to Bud, "we'll hitch up while Paw's gittin' on his things." They rolled back the door of the Hunters' big barn and stepped inside. Cal was carrying the lantern. "We'll take Big Bess," he said. "There's her harness on that right-hand peg. Why—what in thunder—"

The boy was standing behind the row of horse-stalls, his face white and startled. "Look there!" he choked. "Bess is gone, too!"

Certain it was that the big roan mare's sleeping-quarters were empty. The boys rushed back to the house and encountered Myron Hunter just coming out. At the news he took the lantern and ran to the barn himself. A quick examination showed that all the other horses were present.

The farmer's face was grave as he returned to the house. "Best work-horse I ever owned," he said. "I wouldn't have taken six hundred for her. An' that fool dog Shep had to run away again just when he could have been some good." Once more he telephoned the Riverdale police.

By the time the dawn was reddening over the shoulder of the mountain the whole countryside, from Mad River to the Caterwaul, knew that horse thieves had visited their neighborhood. Such news spreads fast among the hill farms. By eight o'clock there were thirty men at the crossroads store, afoot or in their cutters. Most of them carried shotguns.

Sheriff Gardner arrived and took charge of organizing the posses. The men were divided into three groups. One of them, led by John Mason, started eastward to scour the roads leading toward the Maine state line. A second, in charge of Myron Hunter, was dispatched in a westerly direction. And the sheriff himself, in a shiny cutter drawn by his famous pair of black trotters, Kit and Nellie, went north with half a dozen picked men, to head the thieves off if they tried to escape into Canada. The authorities in Riverdale had promised to guard the roads that led south.

Neither Bud nor Cal went to school that day. Cal accompanied his father, seated proudly in the sleigh with his rifle across his knees. Bud stayed at home to care for the stock and keep the fires in Uncle John's absence. Once or twice during the day he went out to the lane behind the barn and studied the tracks leading to the road. The man—there was only one, he was sure—had worn ordinary heavy boots with hobnails. Not a very big foot—about a size eight, he judged. That would fit in with his theory.

In the maze of tracks by the road he thought he could trace the hoof-prints of three horses. Cedar's he knew. He would recognize those specially balanced racing-shoes anywhere. Another was big and broad and heavily calked, a typical winter work-shoe print. And there were still other tracks, blurred and indistinct but apparently smaller than Cedar's, and of a different style of shoe. Bud could not be sure; it might be purely imagination; but when he tried to form a mental picture of the animal that had made those hoof-prints he seemed always to see a little bay mare.

It was after dark that night when Uncle John and the others returned. They had covered nearly fifty miles of main roads and byways, searching every patch of woods where the thieves might have hidden. They and their horses were worn out.

"No word yet from the sheriff," said Uncle John wearily as he pulled off his boots. "He might've picked up their trail. And o' course if they head fer the big cities the chances are the police'll catch 'em. I ain't ready to give up hope yet."

Bud saw Cal on the school barge next morning. The search of the westbound party had also been fruitless, it seemed.

"Listen, Cal," said Bud. "You know who I think did it, of course. Tell me—did you go anywhere near the Hartley place?"

"Sure," Cal replied. "Went right up the Danford road, an' I got 'em to turn in on that wood trail. The stable was empty an' had been fer days. No sign of any fresh tracks. Paw was sore at me fer wastin' time."

The days that followed dragged miserably for Bud. An occasional report would come in, announcing a clew or giving a description of a suspect. But always the hopes thus established were blasted when the next wire arrived. As the week drew to its end Uncle John resigned himself to the loss of his colt. "It's no use now, Bud," he said. "We might as well fergit it an' be as cheerful as we can. As fur's gittin' the cash fer those taxes on your property goes, Cedar probably couldn't have won anyway. An' I've still got hopes o' raisin' the thousand some way or other. Don't you worry yourself."

Bud was worrying, but not about the taxes. He had a feeling that there might still be a way of finding the horse thief and recovering Cedar and Big Bess. And he could not rest as long as the possibility remained untried. What he must do first was to find the gypsy boy, Yance. And he did not want to tell Uncle John about it for fear of getting the lad into trouble.

When he saw Cal at school and suggested a Saturday trip to Leather City he was disappointed to find that his chum would have to spend the day at home. Myron Hunter was going to town for a horse to replace the stolen Bess, and Cal was needed on the farm. There was nothing for it but to go alone.

After the chores were out of the way on Saturday Bud set out. He had made guarded inquiries about the road to Leather City. It was five miles away on the far slope of Hogback Mountain. When Bud had gone a few hun-

159

dred yards he heard a patter of feet and turned to see Tug limping after him. The terrier had a cut in one of his hind feet, and Bud knew the long hike would be too hard for him. By a deal of coaxing and whistling he persuaded Tug to return to the house with him and shut the dog in the shed. Then he started once more.

The road across the mountain was rough and deeply rutted, and it was almost noon when Bud came over the brow of a hill and saw a dreary plain of stunted oak and scrub pine stretching before him. Half hidden in the trees were a dozen scattered houses. The boy felt something hostile in the air of the place. Whistling to keep up his courage, he walked on till he reached the first shack. A bare-headed child in ragged clothes rose from the step and looked at him with dull, scared eyes. He could not tell whether it was a boy or a girl.

"Hi," he called, and smiled with as much friendliness as he could muster. The child made no answer. It looked ready to run at any moment, and Bud did not dare come any closer. "Listen," he said. "Do you know where a boy named Yance lives?"

The youngster nodded its unkempt head and pointed a chapped, grimy hand across the road to another house.

"Thanks," said Bud. The building indicated was a board shanty with sod piled around the foundations and a roof that slumped crazily in the middle. Bud went to the door and rapped with his knuckles. The knocking was hardly louder than the thumping of his heart as he waited.

After a long delay he heard feet shuffling over the floor inside. The door was opened a little way, and a frowsy woman in a faded wrapper scowled out at him.

"Is—is Yance here?" he asked.

"Who be you?" the woman retorted in a husky whisper.

"I'm a friend o' his—Bud Martin," he explained.

At that her expression seemed to change. "Be you the boy 'at give him somep'n' to eat an' a sweater?" she asked. Bud nodded. "Here," she said cautiously, glancing behind her into the house, "come through this way."

Bud entered and found himself in a foul-smelling room, the floor of which was littered with dirt and filth. Across a straw mattress in a corner sprawled a huge man, his mouth open, snoring drunkenly. One glimpse of his face told Bud it was Yance's father. They tiptoed through the room and into a second chamber beyond. Lying on another straw pallet, wrapped in a ragged quilt, Bud saw the gypsy boy. His skin looked drawn, and his black eyes were bigger than ever in his thin face.

"He's been sick," said his mother in her spiritless whisper.

Bud leaned down over the bed. "Hello, Yance," he grinned.

"Hi, Bud," answered the gypsy lad. "What you comin' over here for? Paw's bad today. He might hurt you."

"Oh, I just wanted to see you," said Bud. He could not talk while the woman stood at his elbow. After a moment of awkward silence he asked Yance how he got sick. The boy didn't know. He guessed from being cold and not having anything to eat. Ever since he had been home he had "had hot and cold spells and been weak as a cat."

There was another pause while Bud tried to think of something to say. Then a groan came from the sleeper in the next room, and the floor creaked as if he had started to rise. The woman muttered a frightened exclamation and tiptoed through the door.

The instant her back was turned Bud leaned eagerly toward Yance. "Listen," he said. "Where did Harko Dan go to last week?"

Yance looked scared. "I'll tell you," he whispered. "But don't, fer gosh sakes, let anybody know I told! They'd skin me alive." His voice sank so low Bud could barely hear. "He—he went to Boston," Yance breathed.

At that instant the woman reappeared. "You got to clear out—quick!" she said. "He's wakin' up, an' he's allus worst then. Here—don't go through where he is! You'll have to git out the back! An' look out fer the dogs."

Bud bade Yance a hurried farewell and was steered by the boy's mother through a smelly, dark little passage to a rear door. As he emerged into the gray winter daylight there was a sudden growl at his heels, and up sprang a big, ugly-looking black dog. Bud jumped in spite of himself, and the cur followed, snarling, keeping just out of range of the boy's boot.

Bud reached the road and tried to find a club or a stone. The snow covered everything, and the only missiles he could see were broken bits of ice. He hurled two or three of these at the mongrel, but it still prowled after him, and after a moment its steady snarling brought another dog, quite as mean-looking and even larger than the first.

Till then Bud had merely been annoyed. Now he began to be worried. Threatening gestures had no effect on the brutes. They charged closer and closer, seeming to gain courage from his defenselessness. Once or twice the click of snapping teeth came very close to his calves. He was forced to walk backward to guard against their persistent attacks, and when he reached the edge of the settlement and started up the hill they stayed with him, growing bolder at every step.

Bud was desperate. He stood still, facing the curs, and at that moment there was a sound of pattering feet behind him. Another dog! He whirled to meet it, and his heart gave a bound. There, limping on three weary legs, came that grim warrior, Tug! Panting and winded as he was, the white terrier hesitated not a second but leaped straight at the nearest of the two mongrels.

Bud had confidence enough in his dog to feel that he could take care of himself even against such odds. Now was his opportunity. The woods were only fifty yards away. Racing across the snow, the boy was in among the trees in a moment. He knew exactly what he wanted, and there it was—a two-inch birch sapling. He whipped out his jack-knife, severed the stick with half a dozen furious strokes, and trimmed away the top and branches while he ran back. By the time he regained the road he had a heavy club, four feet long.

The air was full of the hoarse, choking snarls of the battle, punctuated with an occasional high-pitched yelp as Tug's teeth got home on one or another of his enemies. Bud rushed up to the swirling mass of dogs and swung his club hard and accurately. He smote one of the curs such a blow on the skull that it fell stunned. The other had secured a hold on Tug's hind leg, but as Bud raised his stick to strike, the bull terrier's huge jaws came together over the mongrel's loins. It was a terrible grip, like a vise grinding shut on the dog's spine. Tug lifted him off the ground and snapped him downward with one terrific shake. The dog gave a moan and dropped paralyzed in the bloody snow.

Bud cast a hasty glance toward the village. As yet there was no sign of life among the inhabitants, but he expected trouble at any instant.

"Come on, boy," he urged and seized Tug's collar. The terrier seemed willing enough to obey, but his hind leg was dragging and he was more red than white, with blood dripping from half a dozen wounds. There was no time to rest. Bud picked the heavy dog up in his arms and stumbled up the hill at a run. When he was over the crest he put Tug down, and they moved homeward at the best pace they could manage.

It was a long, hard trek for the dog. Bud stopped often to let him rest, and he kept a sharp watch over his shoulder, but there was no pursuit from the folk of Leather City. As they walked Bud was thinking hard. A wild sort of plan was forming in his mind.

"Tug, old boy," he said, as they climbed the last hill, "you'd give a heap, I'll bet, to go with me where I'm going. But now you're laid up, and you'll have to stay right at home. I'm going to miss you, too."

Aunt Sarah saw them coming into the yard and rushed to the door, full of solicitude. She had grown very fond of the big, quiet fighting dog.

"Land o' Goshen!" she cried. "What happened? Did one o' those autos hit him?"

Bud explained that Tug had been set upon by two strange dogs, and let it go at that. Together they bathed his wounds and rubbed them with tallow. The hind leg was not broken, but it needed rest to heal properly. Bud fastened the terrier with a chain to keep him from running about, put new straw in his box, and gave him a well-earned dinner.

"I never saw such a dog!" said Aunt Sarah. "I opened the shed door just a crack, an' he went scramblin' through quicker'n a weasel. He'd been restless ever since you went off this mornin'."

Bud, too, was restless during the next twenty-four hours. Sunday afternoon he went to his room and tied up a little bundle of clothes which he slipped into his book-bag.

At breakfast Monday morning Uncle John lacked his usual cheerfulness. "I saw the sheriff yesterday," he said. "No word about the hoss thieves. They got clean away, I guess."

Bud flushed a little. "Oh, you can't tell," he said. "We might hear some news any day. Well," he continued, rising, "I've got to start for school. Good-by." He hesitated a second, then went to Aunt Sarah and kissed her. "Good-by," he stammered again, and darted out.

decent care. I'll ask 'Paw. Mebbe he can get the sheriff
to fix it."

Bud had left his books in Cal's keeping and gone down
to the bank. There he drew twenty dollars from the savings account he had started two years before with his
muskrat money. The ticket agent at the station did not
know him, and he had got his ticket to Boston without
having to answer any questions.

XV

AT TEN o'clock that February morning Bud was
aboard the Boston train. There was no shivering
in empty box-cars on this journey. Instead he sat in state
on the stuffy plush cushions of a day coach and stared
out the window at white farms and dark forests.

On the way to school in the barge he had had a long
talk with Cal, and confided to him his plan.

"I'm just following a hunch that it was Harko Dan
who stole those horses," he had told his chum. "Yance
says he went to Boston. If he's there, and either Cedar
or Bess is with him, I might be able to find them. And I
can do it better by myself. I want you to give Uncle
John this note when you get home tonight. He won't
like my running off like this, but he'd never have let me
go alone; so I had to.

"There's one other thing," he had added as they neared
the school grounds. "Young Yance is sick—real sick.
We've got to do something to get him out of there."

"You're doggone right," Cal had nodded soberly.
"The kid ought to be some place where they'd give him

167

decent care. I'll ask Paw. Mebbe he can get the sheriff to fix it."

Bud had left his books in Cal's keeping and gone down to the bank. There he drew twenty dollars from the savings account he had started two years before with his muskrat money. The ticket agent at the station did not know him, and he had got his ticket to Boston without having to answer any questions.

The boy had no illusions about the task before him. He knew that the chances were at least ten to one against his locating either the gypsy or the horses. Whoever it was that had stolen them had shown himself to be resourceful and daring. And Boston—supposing that was where they had been taken—was a big place. Bud had forgotten quite how big. As he emerged from the North Station into the roar and bustle of the streets he had a moment of dismay, when he wished himself back in Riverdale.

As he walked along through the hurrying crowds, the geography of the city began to come back to him. He found himself taking the right turnings by instinct. For a while he considered taking a trolley or the elevated, but he was afraid they might confuse him and make him lose his bearings. So mile after mile he trudged on afoot.

It was well into the afternoon when Bud reached his old haunts in South Boston, and he was hungry. Down a side street the familiar yellow shape of a lunch wagon caught his eye, and there unchanged stood Dinty's Diner.

The boy turned toward it with alacrity. The hour was a slack one for trade, and inside the warm, smelly little eating-place Bud found Dinty polishing the nickel coffee urn and whistling an Irish jig.

The lad took a seat on one of the high stools and waited till the proprietor faced about. "Hi, there!" he greeted Dinty with a grin. The little Irishman did not recognize him. "Yes, sir," he replied, politely but with no light of recollection in his eye. "Something to eat?"

"I'll take the same as last time," said Bud with a twinkle. "Coffee and doughnuts, and two cents' worth of something for the dog. Don't you know me, Dinty?" The man stared, thoughtfully rubbing his hand up and down the white apron. Then joy illumined his face.

"Why, it's me little friend Bud!" he cried. "The saints be praised! An' where have ye been at, this long while, Buddy? Faith an' ye're so big an' husky I'd niver know ye fer the scrawny lad ye was."

Between bites of doughnut and sips of coffee Bud unfolded the tale of his adventures. As he ended Dinty's eye was moist. "Ah, 'tis a fine life, the farm life!" he nodded. "Ye put me in mind o' the green hills o' County Clare. An' now ye want to know about a gypsy an' a pacin' colt."

He scratched his bald head dubiously. "Sometimes I hear o' such things," he said at length. "All sorts o' folk comes in here to eat. But there's been no talk of a sorrel pacer. Ye might pick up a word around the stables, though. Yer ould pal Rafferty likes to drive good horses, I know. An' he ain't carin' much where he buys 'em. They'll niver guess who ye are at the Bull's Head. Drop by there an' keep an ear open."

Bud thanked him, paid for his food, and went on in the direction of the stables. In spite of Dinty's assurance that he would not be recognized he hesitated a little before entering the familiar door. The memory of his flight was still too vivid. However, there was no sign of Rafferty about, and the boy walked in unmolested. It was late afternoon, but the teams had not yet begun to return from the day's work, and the place was quiet. A stableman roused up from his nap in a pile of straw and blinked at Bud sleepily.

"Is Joe around?" the boy asked.

"Joe who?" was the reply.

"He used to have charge here in the daytime," Bud explained.

"Naw, he ain't been here fer more'n a year," said the stableman, and relapsed into the straw.

Bud wandered on. The long rows of stalls and the pungent horsy smell of the place brought back the old days sharply. He peered up at the dingy metal plates, tacked above each stall, and read familiar names—Buck, Harry, Prince, Fritz, Jack and Jill, Pompey.

There came a rumble of wheels in the wagon shed. The stableman stumbled to his feet and turned on the lights. In a moment the horses began trampling in, eager for their oats. Two or three teams were driven in—horses and teamsters that Bud did not know. Then came a trio

of mighty iron grays, and the boy's heart bounded. Sure enough, behind them walked the tall, slouching figure of Long Bill Amos.

"Who the Sam Hill—" muttered the big driver when Bud approached him. "Wal, I'll be durned if it ain't Tom Martin's boy—growed up! How be ye, son?"

Bud helped him take the heavy work-harness off his Percherons and give them their feed. Then, at Bill's suggestion, they went out to supper together. "Since you ain't made other arrangements you jest come home an' sleep at my roomin'-house," he said. "An' don't skip out on me this time like you done once before."

At supper for the second time that day Bud told the story of his journey to New Hampshire and the new home he had found there. When he came to describing Cedar and his speed on the snow path, Long Bill leaned forward in rapt attention.

"Boy, how I'd like to see 'em step again!" he exclaimed. "New Hampshire ain't much of a state compared to Maine, but I'll admit they know somethin' about snow racin'. You're goin' to give this colt a chance in the brushes this winter, ain't you?"

Bud's face fell. "That's just why I'm down here," he said. "The colt's been stolen." And he told of Cedar's disappearance and his reasons for suspecting Harko Dan.

"Hm!" mused Amos. "I wonder, now. Jest yesterday I heard Rafferty makin' some sort of a brag about a pacer. I didn't pay much attention, but it was a pacer, I'm sure. Ye might find somethin' out by watchin' Rafferty. Tell ye what we'll do. Tonight I'll take ye down to Red Rooney's bar. The boss generally goes in there fer a chat with the boys in the evenin'. We might hear a word dropped that would give us somethin' to work on."

They finished their meal and strolled down the gas-lit street. At the second corner was a good-sized saloon, from which the sound of a mechanical piano issued loudly. "Look," said the lanky teamster, "there's Rafferty's rig hitched outside."

Bud saw a glistening new cut-under buggy with a bay trotter, blanketed, between the shafts. His heart was beating hard as they passed through the swinging doors into the heat and noise of the saloon. There at the long bar stood his old enemy, drinking with a group. Rafferty gave Amos a casual nod. His glance rested momentarily on Bud, but obviously he did not connect the big, bronzed farm boy with the pale urchin on whom he had once sworn vengeance.

"Come on," muttered Long Bill and led the way to a small table in an inconspicuous corner. He ordered beer for himself and ginger ale for Bud, and they sat quietly sipping their drinks while the place gradually filled. Both of them were listening with all their ears, but above the raucous noise of the piano and the laughter of the patrons they could catch only an occasional phrase of Rafferty's talk.

They had been there perhaps a quarter of an hour when a youth entered and spoke to the bartender nearest the door. "Hey, Rafferty," called the mixer of drinks, "somebody outside wants to see you."

The stable owner downed his whisky, thumped the man next him on the back, and swaggered toward the door with a loud "S'long, boys."

Amos looked at Bud. "We can't leave too close after him, but we'd better mosey out there in a minute," he said. They waited for what seemed a fitting interval and then paid their check and went leisurely out. It was none too soon. Rafferty had taken the blanket off the bay and was in the driver's seat. Another man was just climbing up beside him. As the street light fell for an instant across the face of the stranger Bud's fingers seized Long Bill's arm. "Gosh," he whispered. "It's Harko Dan!"

"What! The gypsy?" asked the Maine man, startled.

"Yes, I'm sure of it," Bud answered. "That overcoat made him look different, but when I got a look at his face I knew him."

The buggy had already started down the street at a smart trot. Bud and his friend ran after it, keeping in the shadow as much as possible. At the end of three blocks Bill was winded.

"Go on after 'em," he puffed. "Keep 'em in sight if ye can!"

Bud sped forward, following the gleam of the brightly polished buggy, now more than a block ahead. Soon he saw Rafferty swing the trotter into a side street. When he arrived at the corner, panting, he saw the stable-keeper's rig standing by the entrance of a dark alley a little way down the street.

Bud waited till Long Bill came up, and they walked cautiously along the pavement to the alley. The street they were in was narrow and badly lighted, but as they neared the buggy they could see that the seat was empty. Amos waited a moment, then thrust his head past the corner and peered into the dark cavern of the alley.

"Huh!" he muttered. "Look a' there, Bud."

The boy took his turn at the edge of the wall and caught a glimpse of two shadowy figures outlined by the flare of a match far down the alley. There was a faint noise like a key grating in a lock, and then a door opened. The two men vanished inside, and the door was shut again.

"Let's wait fer 'em to come out," said Long Bill. "I want to git a look at this hoss-stealin' gypsy."

They strolled back to the end of the street and took their stand where a lighted store window promised a good view of any passing vehicle. After a few minutes there was a sound of hoofs, and the trotter came slowly back up the side street. Huddled in the shadow they waited, breathless, till the buggy was directly opposite.

As the light illumined the features of its occupants Amos pursed his lips in a silent whistle. "So that's him," he said when the rig had passed. "That dark-faced feller with the earrings. Say, listen, I'd swear I saw him this mornin' down to Whelan's blacksmith shop. There was a sorrel hoss in there too, come to think of it."

"Honest?" cried Bud, excited.

"Yeah," said Long Bill. "A good-lookin' hoss with two white stockin's up to his hocks behind, an' a white star in his forehead."

"No," interrupted Bud sadly. "That's not Cedar. There isn't a white hair on him."

"Now wait a jiffy," the Maine man cautioned. "You said somethin' about a big roan drafter bein' stole at the same time. Well, Whelan was shoein' a red roan work-mare when I passed by. She was a beauty too. Caught my eye right off."

Bud shook his head. "I don't believe those were the horses," he said. "Cedar and Bess were both sharp-shod. He wouldn't be taking them to the blacksmith."

"Oh, yes, he might," Bill replied. "Sometimes they change the shoes on a stolen hoss so he won't be so easy to trace. Whelan's thick with Rafferty, too. He'd be just the one they'd go to. Say, kid, now that they're out o' sight, what say we ease ourselves down that alley an' see what sort of a place they went in?"

They walked back to the entrance of the dark, narrow way, looked up and down the street to make sure they were not observed, and went in. Their steps echoed eerily from the walls of the alley, and it was so dark that Bud kept his hands in front of him, groping along in Bill Amos's wake. At last they reached the door where Rafferty and his companion had entered. There were no steps —merely a low sill, less than a foot from the ground.

The teamster tested the heavy iron latch, gingerly at first, then with all his strength.

"It's locked, right enough," he said and laid an ear against the door. Suddenly he lifted his hand. "Listen!" he whispered. Bud followed his example and heard very faintly through the thick oak a familiar sound—the snuffle and stamp of a horse.

"Hear that?" said Bill. "It's some kind of a secret stable, as sure as ye're born."

"Yes, it looks like it," Bud answered. "Do you suppose there's another entrance on the far side?"

"Might be," said the teamster. "Let's go 'round there an' see."

They skirted the block till they came to the opposite entrance of the alley and went in. Sure enough there was a door at the end, similar to the one they had first discovered. This one, too, was stoutly locked, and when Bill lit a match they saw from the dust and débris lodged in the crevices that it had not been opened for a long time.

"If that gypsy friend o' yourn stole the hosses this is where they're keepin' 'em," said Amos as they retraced their steps. "Only how in time are we goin' to find out? Ye wouldn't want to call the police into it without havin' more proof—'specially since Rafferty's mixed up in it. He's got a lot o' political pull."

The problem was still puzzling Bud hours later when he lay tossing on an improvised cot in Long Bill's room.

At last when his big teamster friend had been snoring for a long time an idea flashed into the boy's mind. "I've got it!" he whispered exultantly. "I'll do it the first thing in the morning." And rolling over, he was sound asleep inside of two minutes.

XVI

O F NECESSITY Long Bill Amos was an early
riser. When a teamster was sober he was supposed
to have his dray on the street by seven o'clock. That
meant getting up at five-thirty, and it was exactly that
hour when the lanky Maine man shook Bud awake.

The boy pulled on his clothes, gave himself a hasty
wash, and accompanied Bill to the lunch room for coffee
and "ham-and." As they finished Bud asked his friend
where he would find Whelan's blacksmith shop.

"It's right on the way to the stable," Long Bill replied.
"I'll show ye."

The smithy was an inconspicuous little place on a back
street. As they passed it Bud paused. "I think I'll hang
around here a few minutes," he said. "How long before
you'll be leaving the stable?"

"It'll take half or three-quarters of an hour to git the
team curried an' harnessed," Bill answered. "I'll wait fer
ye." And he walked on, leaving the boy standing on the
curb.

Bud put his hands in his pockets, slouched back to the
wall of the building, and started whistling. To any

passer-by he was simply a neighborhood idler sunning himself against the dingy bricks. Two big horses led by a white-haired old man came up the street, their hoofs clattering on the cobbles.

"Hey!" shouted the ancient. "Open up, Mike, an' let me in."

There was a slow step inside, and the sliding door rolled back. A big Irishman with bushy black eyebrows and huge hairy arms stood in the opening, looking up and down the street. He wore the leather apron of the black-smith's trade.

"Bring 'em in, Hank," he growled. The old man clucked to his team, jerking on their halters, and they went lumbering in. After them, yawning with affected boredom, strolled Bud. As the smith pushed the door shut he cast a sharp glance at the boy.

"What do you want, kid?" he asked gruffly.

"Oh, nothin'," replied Bud, trying to sound as stupid as possible. "I just want to get warm a minute."

He wandered back toward the forge and held his hands before the glowing coals. Apparently Whelan was satis-fied, for he said no more but set about shoeing the horses. Bud let his eye rove over the disorderly array of tools and pieces of old iron that littered the floor of the shop. In a dark corner lay a heap of discarded horseshoes. And when, a moment later, the blacksmith came over to the forge to start an iron heating, it was to this corner that the boy retreated.

Whenever Whelan turned his back Bud's eyes searched the pile of shoes feverishly. Once or twice he shifted his position and contrived to kick some of them off the top of the heap. Most of the shoes were clumsy, broad affairs such as the drafters wore on the city cobbles. But in the midst of them Bud's keen eye at last discovered a slender oval of bright iron. Only part of it was visible, but that part showed a sharp winter toe-calk and a welded build-up plate on the left side.

Bud's heart began to pound like a trip-hammer. He had seen that shoe made, he was almost positive. For what seemed an eternity he had to wait while Whelan was working near by. Then for a moment the burly smith went around to the far side of the horse. Like a flash Bud stooped and picked up the light shoe. There was no time to examine it before Whelan reappeared, but the boy was able to slip it into the side pocket of his mackinaw unobserved.

He stood there a little longer, then yawned and stretched as convincingly as he could, and started slowly toward the door. His hand was just reaching for the catch when the blacksmith's voice sounded, rough and grating, behind him—"Wait a minute, kid!"

Bud froze in his tracks, then turned slowly around. Whelan was scowling at him from under his ferocious black brows. To the boy, trying to return that stare boldly, and measuring his chances of escape, the time seemed long before the blacksmith spoke. "Want to earn two bits?" asked Whelan at last. Bud almost fell over backward in his surprise.

"Sure," he managed to croak through dry lips.

"Here," said the smith, pulling a grimy envelope out of his trousers pocket. "Run up to the Bull's Head Stables and give this to Rafferty. Put it in his hands. If he ain't there, bring it back."

Bud's presence of mind had returned. "All right," he answered, "only gimme the quarter."

"Nothin' doin'," growled Whelan. "Ye'll git it whin ye come back—not until."

Bud took the envelope and opened the door. As he closed it again behind him he heard the smith's hammer ringing on iron. He would not be watched. Whistling to cover his excitement, he hurried up the street and a block from the stable ducked behind a convenient billboard. There he took from his pocket the horseshoe he had picked up from the pile in the shop and examined it eagerly. There could be no question about it. The shoe had been taken from Cedar's left fore foot. Even the faint "C. O." that Cale Otis stamped in the upper surface of all the plates he made was plainly visible.

Putting the shoe back in his pocket, Bud next looked at the envelope he had been commissioned to give Rafferty. Under ordinary circumstances he would not have dreamed of opening it. This case was different. He was tracking a horse-thief, and the note might be an important clew. He found the envelope was sealed only in one

spot, and by careful manipulation he was able to raise
the flap without tearing it. Inside he found a sheet of
coarse paper on which the following memorandum was
crudely spelled out in lead pencil:

CHANGEING SHOES
ON 2 HORSES $25.00
(SORL & RONE)

Twenty-five dollars! Rafferty had to pay high for his
shady work. Bud replaced the bill in its envelope and
went on toward the stable. He did not enter by the office
door, however. Instead he went back through the wagon
shed, now bustling with early morning activity, and
hastened to the quarters of Long Bill's Percherons. The
big teamster was just giving them a final touch of the
brush before harnessing.

Bud slipped into the stall beside him, out of breath,
his face aglow. "Quick," he whispered, "hitch up and
let's get out of here. It's time we got some action!"

"You learned somethin'?" asked Bill.

Under cover of the partition Bud showed him the shoe.
"One of the colt's," he explained. "I found it down at
Whelan's."

The Maine man gave a whistle. "Good kid!" he
breathed. "Gimme a hand with the breechin' an' we'll be
on the street in a jiffy."

They harnessed rapidly and Bill mounted the high
driver's seat, with Bud beside him. "Don't go past the

183

blacksmith shop," cautioned the boy. "I don't want Whelan to see me just yet. I've got a note he told me to deliver to Rafferty—a bill for twenty-five dollars for changing the shoes on Cedar and Big Bess."

"Haw, haw! Good enough!" roared Amos, slapping his thigh. "Ye've sure got 'em where ye want 'em. Now what's the next move?"

"I want to get to the North Station as quick as I can," said Bud. "I've got to look up trains and get a message through to Sheriff Gardner."

Long Bill nodded approvingly. "I'm goin' right that way, an' I'll take ye there," he said. "Git up, Rufus! G'long, there, Doc!" And cracking his whip, he urged the big grays into a trot.

It still lacked a few minutes of eight o'clock when Bud was landed at the old North Station. "I'll be down here at the freight shed, loadin'," said Bill as the boy jumped down.

Bud spent a moment or two studying the Boston & Maine time-table, then went to the telephone desk and asked the operator to put through a long-distance call to Merriton, New Hampshire. Five minutes later he had Sheriff Gardner on the wire. The sheriff heard his news and let out a bellow of delight that nearly split Bud's ear-drum.

"You bet I'll be down!" he chuckled. "I'm through breakfast, an' I'll make the eight-twenty-five. That's the nine-thirty at Riverdale. Good train. Gets into Boston

184

'round half-past eleven. I'll see if I can get hold o' your uncle, too. You meet us there at the train."

Bud dashed out to find Bill Amos. The giant grays had been backed up to the freight platform, and their driver was busy loading his truck.

"They're coming!" Bud cried. "They'll be here at eleven-thirty."

"Good enough!" said Long Bill. "Now I've got an idea. I been thinkin' what if the gypsy or Rafferty should take the hosses away while we're gittin' ready. Here's what I aim to do. Soon as I git rid o' this load I'll drive in the end o' that street an' let the team stand. Then I can keep watch an' follow 'em if they try anything."

Bud saw him drive off a few moments later and settled

down for a long wait. The hours seemed to drag interminably. Long before eleven-thirty the boy was out in the smoky chill of the train shed, looking up the tracks. When the train steamed in he ducked under the arm of the gate-keeper and flew up the platform to meet the two familiar figures he had seen leaving the smoker.

Uncle John's voice was husky as he greeted Bud and gripped his hand. "We've sure been missin' you, son," he said. "Tell me—is it true you've found the colt?"

"Look!" Bud exclaimed and put the horseshoe in his hand.

"By cracky—that's his!" cried the farmer. "How'd you find this?"

"Hold on, now," laughed Sheriff Gardner as Bud started to pour out his tale. "Some one may hear you an' spoil everything. Wait till we're in a cab."

The sheriff hailed a taxi—a chugging little French car that took the corners on two wheels—and they were whisked through the streets to police headquarters. The chief of police was an old friend of the New Hampshire officer, and the urgency of their errand was soon explained to him. He looked grave when the name of Rafferty came into the story. "He's a big man in politics down there—hard to get anything on him," commented the chief. "But this bill from Whelan certainly points to his being interested in the horses. Now where is this secret stable, do you say?"

Bud told him while he listened attentively. "This boy's

186

a lot better detective than some we've got on the force," the chief grinned. "Now I'm going to give you Lieutenant Jamison and a squad of plain-clothes men and you'll go right down there in a police car. Good luck! I'll see you later."

Jamison was a keen-faced, seasoned policeman in citizen's clothes. He had a businesslike way of doing things. The car was driven within a block of the hidden stable. There Bud got out and went up the street to find Bill Amos. The tall teamster was curled up on the driver's seat of his dray, apparently sleeping, while his grays munched oats from their feed-bags. He sat up as Bud came in sight. "I got here at ten o'clock," said he, "an' nobody's been here since."

"All right," Bud replied. "There'll be two plain-clothes men here watching the stable, and the lieutenant thinks you'd better stay here with them because you know where the entrances are. We're going on up to the Bull's Head after Rafferty."

"All right," said Bill ruefully. "I'd give a week's pay to be there, but I'll be more use here, I reckon."

Two of the detectives got out of the car and strolled over toward Amos's dray, meeting Bud as he returned.

"All quiet?" one of them asked out of the side of his mouth.

"Yes," said Bud and got back into the car.

Except for the stable owner's bay trotter and cut-under, hitched up at the curb, the street was empty when they drove up to the stable. "Rafferty's here, anyhow," said the boy.

They climbed out—Jamison and the other detective, Sheriff Gardner, Uncle John, and Bud—and approached the office. The police lieutenant went in first, followed by the others.

Rafferty was sitting on the counter, hat pushed back, a fat cigar in one gesturing hand. He was talking to another man, unfamiliar to Bud, who sat in a chair opposite him. For a second as they entered a flicker of alarm crossed the stableman's face. Then it assumed its usual hard confidence. He half closed his eyes and stuck the cigar in the corner of his mouth.

"Yeah?" he drawled insultingly. "What do *you* want?"

The lieutenant looked him in the eye. "We'd like to talk to you," he said, "about some horses."

"Horses?" said Rafferty. "Just a minute, that's my telephone." He went into the inside office, closing the door after him. Bud had heard no bell ring, but the policemen seemed disposed to overlook this detail, so the boy kept quiet.

They could hear the mumble of Rafferty's voice, speaking low, over the phone. In about two minutes he returned.

"Oh, yes," he said suavely. "You want to buy some horses or hire 'em?"

"Neither," answered Jamison. "We'd like some information about two horses you bought a few days ago."

Rafferty frowned and shook his head. "I don't remember buyin' any horses lately," he said.

"Perhaps I can refresh your memory," Jamison coun-
tered. "One was a red roan draft mare, about seventeen
and a half hands and fifteen hundred pounds. The other
was a three-year-old colt—sorrel—a pacer."

The stablekeeper showed some heat. "Naw," he cried,
"you're all wrong. I didn't buy 'em. Who the devil are
you, anyway?"

"Headquarters," answered Jamison briefly, displaying
his badge. "These horses were stolen, Mr. Rafferty, and
we had an idea they might have been sold to you. You
won't mind, of course, if we search the place?"

Rafferty's relief was obvious in spite of his injured
air. "It's an outrage!" he stormed. "Sure—go on an'
search. You won't find 'em here. I'm goin' to report this
to the mayor an' have some o' you fresh cops fired off the
force!"

Jamison nodded to the plain-clothes man, who went
out to look through the stable. For the next quarter of an
hour the visitors stood about the office and waited, talking in undertones, while Rafferty alternately fumed and
sulked.

At length the police lieutenant looked at his watch and
walked over to the door. "Here they come," he said
quietly.

There was a rumble of dray wheels outside. From the

window Bud saw Bill Amos guiding his grays up to the front of the stable. With him on the driver's seat were two other men, and a third sat on the tail of the truck, holding the halters of three blanketed horses.

Bud seized Uncle John's arm. "Look!" he cried. "They've got Cedar!" But the next instant his face fell. "No," he stammered in dismay, "it—it isn't Cedar, either!"

For though one of the led horses was unmistakably Myron Hunter's big roan, the middle one—the high-headed young sorrel—had a pair of white hind legs and a diamond-shaped patch of white in the center of his forehead.

XVII

A T THE moment Jamison opened the office door to
step outside Rafferty slipped from behind the
counter and started back toward the stable. He might
have made his escape had not the detective returned just
then from searching the place. Bud saw the stable-keeper
turn reluctantly back into the office as the plain-clothes
man held up a warning hand. Outside other things were
happening. Lieutenant Jamison hailed the policeman
perched on the driver's seat of the truck.

"All right, Bailey," he ordered. "Bring him in here."

Until then Bud had scarcely noticed the center man
of the trio on the dray. It was Harko Dan, his slouch
hat pulled low over his dark, surly face. As the gypsy
clambered down from the seat Bud caught a momentary
gleam of metal between his wrist and that of the plain-
clothes man. They were handcuffed. Followed by Bill
Amos, the pair crossed the sidewalk and came into the
office.

There were a few seconds of silence as Rafferty and

the gypsy stood facing each other. Then Jamison spoke to the stable owner. His tone was low, almost confidential.

"Is this the fellow?" he asked.

At the words the gypsy's anger blazed forth. "Ha-a-a!" he snarled at Rafferty. "You double-crossed me, eh? Well, you're goin' to jail with me, you dirty rat! I'll tell 'em who put up the cash an' who owns that hide-out joint."

Rafferty's florid face had turned a sickly white. All his nonchalance was gone.

"I never saw him before," he bleated, "him or the horses, either! It's a frame-up!"

"Is it?" said Jamison curtly. "How about this?" And he thrust Bud's scrap of paper under the stableman's nose. "It's a bill to you from Whelan for changing the shoes on two of those horses out there—the sorrel and the roan."

Rafferty stared at the paper, unable to speak, and Jamison turned to one of his aides. "All right, Mike," he said, "call the precinct and have 'em send the wagon."

"A mighty good job, Lieutenant," boomed the sheriff, approvingly. "But there's one other little matter that ain't clear yet. Let's take a look at those horses."

Leaving the two prisoners in charge of the detectives, the rest of the party moved outside. Sheriff Gardner pointed to the sorrel colt at the rear of the truck. "John," he said, "your horse didn't have any white on him, did he?"

Mr. Mason stepped closer to the animal in question. "No," he answered, "but here he is just the same. I'd know that colt if he'd been painted white all over. They've doctored him."

Bud could hardly believe his eyes. It was Cedar, beyond question. The young horse recognized them and thrust out his eager velvet muzzle for sugar. The white patches, on close examination, proved to be cleverly stained into the hair with a thin white paint.

Now for the first time the boy's attention fell on the third horse in the group. It was a rangy gray with slim trotter's legs—so light in color that it looked almost white.

"I've seen that horse," cried Bud excitedly. "Harko Dan had him hidden back in the woods on the Danford road."

"Stolen, too, I reckon," said the sheriff. "There was a flier out last fall about a gray trotter that was missin' from over near Keene. I wouldn't be surprised if this was the hoss right here."

The police van rolled up with a clang of gongs, and into it were bundled Harko Dan, grim and silent, and Rafferty, who had recovered his color and was vociferously demanding his rights as a Democrat and a ward leader.

Bud, watching him as he bumped away over the cobbles, remembered the day when Rafferty had threatened to have him locked up. By the irony of fate it was he

—the homeless waif of two years before—who had now brought about the stable owner's arrest.

"All right, gentlemen," said Lieutenant Jamison, "I'll turn over these two horses to you. We'll keep the gray until we can get in touch with the authorities up at Keene and see if he's theirs."

"There's one more thing you may be able to help us settle up," said Uncle John. "This young detective here has been left some property. He can't legally claim it until we can prove his identity. His father was named Thomas Martin, and he was a Boston man—a teamster."

"You don't mean Tom Martin that drove a truck for the Bull's Head Stables?" interrupted Jamison.

"Yes, that was my dad," said Bud.

"Well, what do you think of that!" the lieutenant exclaimed. "When he was a young chap he used to drive a patrol wagon over at the Sixth Precinct. I was walking a beat then. We were regular buddies."

"Did you know him when he married Jane Hartley?" asked Uncle John.

"Yes indeed," said Jamison, "and a fine girl she was."

"That ought to be enough identification," the sheriff put in, "your affidavit an' one from Bill Amos here, provin' that Bud is Tom Martin's boy. We'll have the birth records in a few days, an' then we can take some action. Now, Lieutenant, if you feel the same as I do you're hungry. What do you say we all go get some dinner?"

These words were music to Bud's ears. The breakfast

194

he had eaten at six that morning had not been heavy, for the boy had had too much on his mind to be hungry. And all through the exciting events of the day he had been so occupied with the work in hand that the thought of food had never occurred to him. Now that the job

was finished he suddenly discovered that it was three o'clock and he was ravenous.

The horses were quartered in the Bull's Head and the party started to look for a restaurant. "I know a dandy place," said Bud. "Come on with me." And he led the way toward Dinty's Diner.

Uncle John and the sheriff exchanged a smile when they saw the lunch wagon, but they had no cause to regret

Bud's choice. The little Irish proprietor gave them a royal welcome and soon set before them juicy steak and savory fried potatoes such as he alone knew how to prepare.

While they ate, Bill Amos told the story of Harko Dan's capture.

About ten minutes after the car had driven off, he said, he and the two detectives had seen the gypsy hurrying down the street and into the alley where the stable was hidden. Bill had told the others about the entrance from the opposite side of the block, and one of the plain-clothes men had gone around to guard it at once. After a few moments they heard his police whistle. They ran down the alley, found the door unlocked, and entered the stable. Inside, the stalls were empty, but they went on to the opposite door. Outside in the alley they came upon the three horses and Harko Dan, standing sullenly at the point of the detective's revolver.

"It worked just the way I hoped it would," said Lieutenant Jamison. "I figured Rafferty would try to tip the gypsy off, and we might have a chance to get them both at once and the horses with them."

When the meal was over Bud said good-by to Dinty.

"Begorra, lad, an' I wish ye luck," said the little chef. "An' if the time iver comes that ye're hungry an' lack the price of a meal, mind the diner's always open an' ye're welcome. Here—take this fine bone o' beef to the white dog, bless him!"

They made arrangements with Bill Amos to ship the horses by rail the following day. As they took leave of the Maine man he called Bud aside.

"When did ye say the big race was comin' off?" he asked.

"Washington's Birthday," Bud replied. "You'd better come up and pull for Cedar to win."

"Jest what I was thinkin'," Long Bill said. "Mebbe I need a holiday 'bout that time."

An hour later they boarded a train for the north, and by nine o'clock that night Bud and Uncle John were finishing up the chores.

"Ho hum!" yawned the farmer as they carried their lanterns back to the house. "A long day, but a great day's work! I reckon we'll both sleep sounder tonight than we have since the colt was stole."

And Bud, stopping to fondle the big white terrier and watch him clean the last shred from Dinty's beef bone, agreed that sleep was in order.

XVIII

BUD awoke to find himself something of a hero on the mountain. Farmers along the road greeted him with respect, and children ran to front gates to stare after him. Myron Hunter made him a present of twenty-five dollars as a reward for the recovery of Big Bess, and he was so insistent that Bud had to accept it.

Even in Riverdale he was an object of interest, for the local paper, as well as some of the Boston dailies, carried the story of his part in apprehending the horse thief and bringing Cedar and Bess back to their owners. At school he was really embarrassed by the attention he received, and as soon as possible at noon he and Cal left the building to take a walk downtown.

Riverdale was horse-crazy. The billboards blazed with posters advertising the snow races. And wherever men were gathered along the street the boys could hear discussions of the chances of this or that trotter.

"Don't seem like they'd ever heard o' the one that's goin' to win," snorted Cal. "What a surprise they'll git when ol' Cedar comes sailin' in."

"Gee," murmured Bud, atingle with excitement, "I wonder if he *has* got a chance! Harko Dan must have driven him hard all night and the next night to get to Boston. Maybe this has thrown him off so he won't be in shape. Let's see, how soon is it? Today's the tenth. Gosh, it's less than two weeks to the race!"

But Bud's fears as to Cedar's condition were set at rest next day when the red colt and the roan mare came down the chute from their box-car. Cedar sniffed deeply of the crisp winter air and tossed his fine head high as he pawed the snow.

"Durned if he ain't ready to go right now," chuckled Uncle John. That evening they spent in sponging away the white patches with which the pacer had been disguised. It was a delicate job, particularly on his forehead, for the fumes of the turpentine got into the colt's eyes, and they had to work slowly and carefully.

The next day he had his first work-out since he was stolen, and when Bud came home at night he found Uncle John happy over the form he had shown. "He's a mite nervous yet, o' course," said the farmer, "but I can't see that he's lost any of his speed. I reckon we can sign him up fer the race. How much is the entry fee?"

"Twenty-five dollars," Bud answered. "Here!" And he thrust Mr. Hunter's reward money into Uncle John's hand.

In the busy lobby of Canby's Hotel where the details of the Free-for-All were handled, the entry of "Cedar, sorrel pacing colt; John Mason, owner and driver," created only a mild ripple of interest.

"Oh, yes, that's the one the gypsy stole, isn't it?" said one of the bystanders. "Glad to see you racing, John." And at once he turned back to a fervid argument about the relative merits of two up-state trotters.

Bud and Cal spent every minute they could spare from classes on the street and at the speedway, for the atmosphere of the race was contagious.

A full week before the great event horses and horsemen began to come into the city. Out of beautifully fitted traveling-cars stepped graceful, blanketed trotters with their trainers in close attendance. Big, bluff men in fur coats strolled in and out of the hotel or watched the new arrivals as they were led to the stables. There were little-known entrants from as far away as Hartford and Bangor, and rumors spread rapidly about their speed.

But most of the talk seemed to center about two horses. One was Chocorua, the famous Felton mare, now well into her second winter as undisputed mistress of the Valley speedways. The other was a splendid trotting stallion from Maine that went by the name of Saco Boy and had many backers among wise horsemen who had seen him win races on the half-mile tracks. There was some question about his speed on snow, but all agreed that he had courage.

The meeting was scheduled to extend over two days.

There were to be three trial classes, each racing three heats. The winner in each class would qualify for the three-heat final.

The division into classes was made by drawing lots. Possibly they were fairly cast, but Bud and Cal heard some criticism arising from the fact that all the favorites, with one or two exceptions, were drawn for Classes One and Two, in which the elimination heats were to be raced off on the twenty-first. The winners of these two classes would be sure of an overnight rest before the final. The morning of Washington's Birthday was set for the third-class trial heats, and in the afternoon the championship would be decided.

To the chagrin of the boys they found that Cedar was drawn in Class Three. Bud was considerably upset by this fact until he got home and told Uncle John about it. The farmer took the news philosophically.

"Oh, well," he said, "that ain't really so bad. It may give the colt a better chance to git into the final, because the competition won't be so stiff in that third class. If he comes through in the mornin' I'll trust him to give a good account of himself in the afternoon."

Washington's Birthday that year fell on a Tuesday. As the day approached Bud grew so excited he could hardly eat. The last Saturday before the race was a bustle of preparation. Bud helped Uncle John mend blankets and wash the cutter. He took Cedar down to Cale Otis's

201

smithy and had his shoes tightened. He curried the colt's red sides until his arms ached.

It was during the afternoon, while Mr. Mason was soaping and suppling the best set of harness, that Sheriff Gardner drove past and stopped a moment to chat.

"Hello there, Bud," he boomed cheerily. "How's young Sherlock Holmes today? Say, sonny, I've got some good news for you. Myron Hunter spoke to me about that gypsy boy, Yance, an' I went over to Leather City yesterday. He's better, but he looked so peaked I knew he'd never be real strong with the kind o' care he was gettin' in that shack. So I subpoenaed him as a witness in this horse-stealin' case an' jest brought him along home with me. He's a nice kid. When he gets his strength back he can be a chore boy at my place an' go to school."

Bud was delighted by the news. "Tell Yance as soon as Cal and I have this race off our minds we'll be down to see him," he said.

"That's right," chuckled the sheriff. "You are kind o' busy these days, ain't you? Well, I wish you an' the colt luck." And clucking to his horses, the big-hearted officer drove on down the road.

When evening chore time came Uncle John looked at their work with satisfaction. "I reckon the rig's ready, such as it is," he said. "I've been workin' the colt pretty hard the last few days. Now we can taper off an' give him jest enough on the road to keep him in shape."

He was standing by the big grain chest as he spoke, his

202

right hand resting on its edge. And suddenly the heavy cover, which had not been pushed far enough back, fell with a sickening crash.

Uncle John's face was white as he lifted the cover and pulled out his hand. Bud ran to his side, a sense of catastrophe filling his soul. The farmer was looking at the pitifully crushed fist. He tried to move his fingers and winced with pain. "It's broken," he said dully.

Bud got him into the house and harnessed old Betsy. Half an hour later they reached the doctor's house on the valley road, and Uncle John submitted the crushed hand to an examination.

"Two bones fractured," said the physician. "John, you won't be able to use this hand for a month, and if you don't take mighty good care of it once I get it in splints it'll never be any good."

He set the bones, dressed the bruises, and bandaged the hand tightly over wooden splints while Uncle John sat in stoical silence. It was not until Bud had driven half-way home that the farmer spoke what was in both of their minds. "There goes the race," he said, and Bud nodded miserably. "Unless—" he went on, after a pause —"unless you could drive him yourself."

The boy looked up, startled, an eager light in his eyes. "Gee, Uncle John! Could I?" he asked.

"Yes," the farmer answered, "I believe you could. The colt likes you, an' you've handled him enough to know what he can do. It looks like about the only way out."

On Sunday Bud had the bulk of the work to do, for there were few things that Uncle John could manage with his left hand. In the afternoon they hitched up Cedar to the sleigh and gave him a half hour's pacing on the level road in the valley. Uncle John talked to Bud while he drove, giving him all the advice he could from his own experience.

"Now, Bud," he concluded earnestly, as they came back up the hill, "don't let anybody tell you how to do. Drive your own race. An' don't let 'em cheat you. You've seen enough racin' so that I reckon you know some o' their tricks."

Bud nodded, sober-faced. "I'll do my darnedest," he said. "I guess we need that thousand more than ever now, Uncle John."

The boy worked hard next morning and succeeded in finishing the chores in time to catch the school barge. When Cal heard the news he could hardly contain himself. "Gee whiskers!" he cried. "Maybe I wouldn't like to be you! Durn you, Bud, if you don't beat 'em now, I'll give you a shiner with my own hands."

The two boys rushed out the minute school was over that afternoon and ran all the way to the speedway. When they arrived, panting, at the track, the first race was already over and the opening heat of Class Two had been run. The stands near the finish were fairly well filled, and a crowd lined the track for several hundred yards. At the point which Bud and Cal approached the spectators were more scattered, and they had no trouble getting places in front.

"Who won the first race?" asked Bud of the man next him.

"Who?" he replied with partisan scorn. "Why, Chocorua, of course. Ye didn't think any o' these other nags could give her trouble, did ye? She won in straight heats an' wasn't even pushed."

"What was her time?" Cal asked.

"They say she made the first heat in 2.08," the man answered, "but she could've beaten that, easy. Look"—he pointed up the track—"here comes Saco Boy in the lead! He was second in the first heat. Watch him pull away!"

The big black trotter was coming down like an express train, a length ahead of the field. As he passed, Bud caught a glimpse of his driver hunched forward over the reins—a gray-haired man with a wizened brown face like a russet apple. He knew him! It was Billy Randall, the veteran trainer and driver who had noticed Cedar at the fair.

The Maine stallion continued to draw away from the other horses, and they could tell from the cheering as he crossed the finish-line that he had won.

Slowly the big field was walked back to the start, and after a brief rest, made ready for the last heat. The boys could see the dark dots wheeling into position, then steadying and coming down in a flying line. A puff of smoke, followed by a report, told them the starter's gun had signaled a fair getaway.

This time Saco Boy no longer had things his own way. A fast-looking gray pacer was leading him by a neck as they drew near, and both horses were moving at top speed. Together they flashed by, and they were still together when they neared the stands. A continuous roar came from the spectators. Obviously it was a close finish, and everybody along the track started running toward the judges' stand. When Bud and Cal arrived, the winner's name had been posted.

"Saco Boy," it read. "Time, 2.06."

"Wow!" cried the supporter of Chocorua, who had run down with them. "Won't that be a race? The mare'll show him the way, though. She can trot in 2.06 any time."

The boys got a ride home with a neighbor who had been to see the races, and Cal accompanied Bud up the hill to help him with the evening work. Both of them were rather quiet as they went about their chores.

"Oh, well," said Cal at last, "I know how you feel, but by golly, you won't have to be ashamed o' Cedar, no matter what happens. He's all clear grit, that colt."

"Yes," Bud answered, "he'll do his best, but he's only a baby, really, and—oh, shucks! Well, we'll see what happens tomorrow!"

XIX

BUD got up at four-thirty and dressed, in the bleak dark of that Washington's Birthday morning. The cold and the excitement made him shake all over like a leaf as he went stumbling out into the barn. But he climbed the mow and dug into the hay savagely with the fork to pull himself together. And when he came down Tug was there to give his hand a warm, reassuring lick.

The white terrier was all but well now. Only a few healing scars remained from his encounter with the gypsy dogs, and his limp was entirely gone.

Bud hustled through the work in time to give Cedar a last brushing down, then fed and watered him with care and went in to breakfast. For Aunt Sarah's sake he made a valiant effort to eat, but he was keyed too high that morning to enjoy the taste of food. Uncle John came out with him to help harness, and by eight o'clock they were ready to start. Bud waved good-by to Aunt Sarah and drove the colt out of the dooryard to the musical jingle of bells. Tug went too, sitting erect between their feet.

All down the snowy miles to Riverdale Bud had to check Cedar's pace, soothing him constantly by voice and hand, for the colt felt like skylarking.

"This jog to town is a good thing fer him," Uncle John said. "It'll take some o' the devilment out of him, an' maybe he'll be ready fer business at race time."

At the outskirts of the town they overtook the Hunters' sleigh, in which Cal and his father were riding, and accompanied them to the speedway. There was still nearly an hour before the first heat was scheduled to begin, and Bud blanketed the colt and walked him slowly up and down while the others were getting their tickets for the grandstand. Uncle John reported his injury to the race committee and made the necessary arrangements for having a substitute drive in his place.

The holiday had brought out a far larger crowd than had been present the afternoon before. Not only had many come afoot, but there were rows of cutters ranged along the sides of the track, with an occasional automobile among them. The sky was overcast and the air sharply cold.

"Looks as if it might snow later," said Uncle John, casting a weatherwise eye aloft. He had come back for a last look at Cedar before the race.

A gong began to clang at the judges' stand. "Ten minutes," said Uncle John. "Warm him up a bit back here, then take him up over the course so it won't be strange to him. Good-by, lad."

208

Bud took Cedar's blanket off and let him stretch his legs a trifle on the road back of the stand. When he seemed well limbered up the boy swung his horse to the foot of the speedway and jogged him up past the grandstand. Then along the line of jingling sleighs and pungs he guided Cedar toward the starting-point. There were laughter and a few jeers as they passed—the strong young horse, with his winter coat as smooth as Bud could brush it, but looking a bit rough and uncouth about the legs; the scarred old cutter, its moth-eaten cushions well dusted and its steel runners polished till they gleamed; and sitting very straight under an ancient buffalo robe, the serious-faced boy with his eyes to the front.

Eight horses besides Cedar were moving up to the start. Most of them were local trotters. They had beautiful, clipped legs, and right at their tails—on them, in fact—sat their drivers, in sulky sleighs that were no more than light skeletons of braced steel, with ridiculous little shells of seats above.

As they swung into position Bud looked off down the mile straight-away with a pounding heart. He felt himself in a sort of daze, his arms heavy, helpless. Then almost before he knew it the starting gun had sounded. Ahead of him flew the other eight, close-bunched.

A laugh went up as the boy gritted his teeth and urged the sorrel colt after them. Hot tears of anger filled his eyes. But the swift rhythm of Cedar's haunches under the taut reins brought back his confidence and even a thrill of pride. He steeled himself for the job ahead.

And now from the crowds that lined the snow path came scattering cheers as they went by, for some of the men from the upper end of the county and some of Bud's schoolmates recognized them. Slowly, very slowly, it seemed to the boy, they were coming up—overhauling first one rival and then another, till, as the wire drew close, there were six behind them.

Cedar finished in third place. Bud swung him around to pass the grandstand on the return journey. He could not bring himself to look up. He was red with shame. But there were many good horsemen along the track who had seen the colt's fine spurt and who threw Bud a word of encouragement as he went back for the second heat.

Well, there should be no leaving at the post this time! Bud gathered the reins, and the sorrel picked up speed as he neared the start. Over the line he went like a shot, right abreast of the leaders. Halfway down the track Bud looked sidewise. The winner of the first heat, a game little chestnut gelding named Billy D., was holding even with the boy's sleigh seat, trotting with all that was in him. The rest were trailing behind. Bud thrilled to see the red colt then. As his grip on the reins tightened, Cedar responded, speeding faster and faster, with the wind in his mane, over the hard-packed snow he loved. And he crossed the finish line with a good three lengths to spare.

There was a yell from the crowd as the time went up. Bud looked at the board and nearly choked with surprise

Two-eight, it said. Surely there was a mistake. In a minute they would find it out and change the "o" to a "1." But no, the crowd was still cheering. "Cedar! Cedar!" cried the voices in the stand, hailing a new popular favorite. And flushed this time with pride, Bud grinned up at the throng, trying to find Uncle John and Cal and Tug.

The colt was over his first nervousness now, and Bud let him take plenty of time in going back for the final test. When they reached the start the boy got out of the sleigh and stooped to rub down Cedar's steaming legs with a dry piece of sacking. A man spoke, so close to his shoulder that it startled him.

"Give 'im the whip, this last heat," he said in a low voice. "They're goin' after yuh. That colt's got better time in 'im, yet, an' you'd better use it. Don't look around, but drive like the devil, all the way!" And the man was gone before Bud could open his mouth to reply. The single glimpse he got of him had shown a sallow, thin fellow with a black mustache, wearing a great coonskin coat.

Already the horses were back on the track. Bud was thinking quickly, disturbed by the uncalled-for advice of the stranger. It was true enough that he must do his best to win this last heat, but why had the man been so anxious to tell him so? Was he betting on Cedar? Uncle John's words came back to Bud as distinctly as if he were hearing them spoken: "Don't let anybody tell you how to do. Drive your own race." And the boy resolved that, green as he was in such matters, he would use his own judgment and disregard all outside counsel. Still worrying a little, he swung the big red colt into place above the start.

Down they came, all together, like a cloud before the wind, as the flag dropped.

Cedar was rocking along, smoothly as ever, almost in the center of the group. Suddenly Bud saw two horses moving up, one on each flank, and though less than a quarter of the course was finished their drivers were plying the whip savagely. As the sleighs drew even with Cedar's head both men pulled inward a barely perceptible distance. The colt's flying forefeet were very near to striking their runners.

In another instant he might have broken, for he was disconcerted and tossed back his head. But Bud pulled him far off to the left and spoke to him once or twice as Uncle John would do. The young pacer held his stride and a second later was going again like the wind, outside and nearly abreast of the others.

Beyond the half mile they had passed all but the little chestnut, Billy D. He fought them hard all the way down, but Cedar's mighty strength was too great a handicap. Bud was slacking off on the reins at the finish, and the colt drifted easily under the wire, a length to the good.

The spectators came pouring out of the stand as Bud

guided Cedar off the track. A crowd of curious men and boys surrounded them, staring open-mouthed at the young stallion while Bud wiped down his legs and blanketed him. After a moment Uncle John shouldered through the onlookers, followed by Tug and the Hunters. No words were needed to express the farmer's joy. It glowed in his square, brown face.

"That was drivin', boy!" he said, and gripped Bud's hand. Then he looked around at the crowd. "Here, let's git the colt out o' this an' give him a chance to rest," he added.

In the lee of a pine thicket near the upper end of the speedway they found a sheltered place to tie the horses and eat their lunch. When Cedar was cool enough they gave him a light feed and a little drink.

"What was it happened up there near the start in the last heat?" asked Uncle John as they consumed Aunt Sarah's sandwiches and pie.

"Two of the drivers tried to box me," said Bud, and he went on to tell how Cedar had escaped from the trap. "There was another funny thing happened," the boy remarked. "Just before the last heat a man came and warned me to drive for all I was worth and lay into the colt with the whip. Do you suppose he really meant to help me? I didn't like his looks, so I didn't pay much attention to him."

"He might've wanted Cedar to win," said Uncle John, "but it sounds more to me as if he'd been tryin' to

use the colt up—kill his speed fer this afternoon. Who was the feller?"

Bud described the stranger, but neither Uncle John nor Myron Hunter could remember having seen him.

The next two hours were hard for the youthful jockey. No one talked much. They all took turns at leading the blanketed pacer up and down to keep his legs from stiffening. Now that the first flush of winning the elimination race had passed, Bud had moments of bitter doubt. He thought of the crudeness of their preparations for the final and compared them mentally with what was going on in the big, steam-heated box stalls at the hotel stable, where grooms and trainers were even then putting the last fine touches on Chocorua and Saco Boy.

He thought of Cedar—a raw young colt, driven down that forenoon over ten miles of country road, raced in three hard heats in the morning, and handled clumsily by an amateur driver. What chance had he to win against those famous pets of the racing-game, fresh from a night's rest and maneuvered by wise and tricky hands?

Then he looked up at the big red horse stepping proudly along at his side, saw the courage that glowed in his eye and the strength of his arched neck—and shame filled the boy's heart. Cedar, at least, had no yellow streak.

Two o'clock came, and the young pacer was put back between the shafts of the cutter. Uncle John pulled the last buckle tight with his left hand and gave the colt's cheek a lingering pat. "I guess it's time to go down to the judges' stand," he said. "They'll likely make the three hosses parade past 'fore the first heat."

They led Cedar down the track, still in his blanket, as far as the upper end of the grandstand. There the wraps were taken off and Bud took his place once more in the sleigh while the others climbed to their seats in the pavilion.

There was a great throng gathered at the track that cold, gray afternoon. The Governor had come over from Concord, and by his side in the decorated box loomed the gigantic figure of a famous New Hampshire Congressman who never missed a good harness race if he could help it.

Driving up past the crowds to the judges' stand, Bud realized with dismay that he and Cedar were a part of the spectacle that these thousands had come to watch. Luckily his stage-fright did not pass through the reins into the horse. He was as gay as ever, and even danced a little as the band played.

Close by, their blanketed forms the center of deep knots of men, were the colt's two opponents. Bud watched them as their coverings were stripped off. Saco Boy stood forth magnificent—a great black stallion with fire in his eyes and mighty muscles leaping in his neck and shoulders. He was more massive and even taller than Cedar, but, Bud felt, no better proportioned.

Then his glance shifted to Chocorua. Instantly the old

hatred he had felt when he first saw her returned. It seemed as if no horse had a right to such slim, long racing shanks. She was built like a greyhound, and the similarity was made more striking by her blue roan color and the clipped smoothness of her chest and legs. Her head was long and narrow and wicked. With her ears back she was like a reptile—venomous.

As Bud looked past her his eye was caught by a coonskin coat and a thin, dark-mustached face above it. It was the stranger of the morning, standing close by the mare's head and engaged in an earnest conversation with two men. One was a hard-faced, smallish man in black furs—Andy Blake, the mare's driver. The other was Sam Felton himself. The fat-jowled magnate's eye met Bud's and flashed with recognition. Was it Cal who had said that the Feltons never forgot a grudge? There was something of vindictive triumph in that glance that the boy did not like. And the mystery that had puzzled him was cleared up at last. Instead of a friend the man who had given him the tip was an enemy—one of Chocorua's backers. No wonder he had urged Bud to drive the colt to a needless whipping finish in the morning race. Perhaps it was he who had engineered the attempt to box Cedar, as well. The boy thanked his stars he had followed Uncle John's advice.

From the judge's booth sounded the sharp, impatient banging of the gong. "Ten minutes!" came the call, and Bud gathered the reins once more for action.

216

XX

BUD took Cedar on a little warm-up spin along the track, then came back with the others to the judge's stand. There was another laugh at the rude racing turn-out from Red Horse Hill, for many people in the crowd had not been present that morning. Andy Blake, mounted close behind the tall hind-quarters of his mare, grinned spitefully at Bud's reddening face. But old Billy Randall, who held the reins over Saco Boy, gave the lad a friendly nod.

"Sorry 'bout John gittin' hurt," he said, "but you drove a good race this mornin'. That's a great youngster you've got there."

From the judges' stand the horses' and drivers' names were read out and the conditions of the race announced. Three heats were to be driven and the championship decided on points if no horse won twice. As the announcer put down his megaphone a babel of sound rose from the stands—cheers and shouts of encouragement. The three drivers turned their horses' heads and jogged slowly up the track toward the start.

Bud had an entirely different feeling from the one with which he had entered the morning race. He was alert and tense now, determined to fight. They swung around at the head of the snow path and got under way. Nearing the start the big, black trotter flashed out ahead, fiercely impetuous. He left the line a good four lengths beyond the others, and Bud expected to hear the jangling of the recall bell. Instead came the report of the gun, and the starter's flag fell. In spite of an outcry from the crowd and the wild gesticulations of Andy Blake the heat was on.

A great excitement entered Bud's veins. His grip on the reins tightened, and he shouted to Cedar through the whipping wind. The colt was pacing swift and sure as in the forenoon, one pointed ear cocked back for Bud's voice, the other forward. Chocorua's evil head, close by their sleigh-seat at first, dropped back and back till Bud could see her no longer, and the colt drew up little by little on the great trotting stallion.

It was such a finish as horsemen dream of. Scarcely half a length apart down the last quarter fought the sorrel and the black. There was so little to choose that many called it a dead heat. But with the sting of Randall's whip on his shining side, Saco Boy flung himself under the wire a nose ahead.

"Two-five and a quarter!" bawled the timekeeper. And as Bud came out of the spell of the race he realized that thousands of voices had been calling on Cedar to win.

Again the long mile back to the starting-point, and then a little breathing-spell as they got ready for the second heat. Blake, sullen and resentful, had saved his mare after the uneven start. She stood there, poised on her slim legs, hardly breathing as yet, while the black stallion puffed and pawed and flung white spume flecks back over his ebony neck. Cedar was quieter, but the exertions of the day had begun to tell on him. His deep sides rose and fell with the effort he had made. Bud soothed him with pet names and rubbed him unceasingly as they stood waiting.

It had begun to snow when the starter called them out —long, slanting darts of white hurled across the track by the keen north wind.

They brought their horses to the right about and came down to the post again. The tall roan mare leaped to the front this time, with Randall and Bud driving close at her heels. Blake was not lagging now. From the start he drove her—drove her with hard hand and hard voice, the whip ever poised above her lean back. And still, as she fled away, came Cedar after her, eager as a hawk, his swift feet thudding on the firm-packed snow. Off to the right the great black horse held the pace for a while, then burst into a thunderous gallop, and they left him and sped on.

It was a terrific gait the mare was making. And she held it to the end, for Blake began using the whip at the three-quarter post and brought her in under a flying lash. Gallantly Cedar followed, but at the finish there was still a length that his weary legs could not make up.

Bud had to shut his jaw hard, for he wanted to cry as he stood by Cedar's side after that second heat. There was a faint, constant trembling in the steel muscles under the colt's damp hide and his coat was bright no longer, but dark with sweat. Rubbing and working at those beautiful legs as if his life depended on it, the boy talked to him breathlessly, pleading with him, begging forgiveness for the one last trial that Cedar must endure. Twice he had given his best and lost. The race and the purse were gone, of course—utterly beyond their reach, but Bud knew they must keep on and see it through.

When he looked up for a moment men were jumping in the air in excitement, shouting and pointing toward the judges' pavilion. On the board were figures which at first Bud read without believing. They said: "2.04."

Then at his elbow he saw Billy Randall standing. The old trainer's voice was queer and husky as he spoke.

"I wanted to look at that colt o' yours, lad," he was saying. "I guess we're through—Saco Boy an' I. Once he breaks in a race he's done for the day. But you've got the greatest snow horse in New England there under that blanket—"

"Ye're durn right!" interrupted a voice behind them, and Bud turned quickly to see Long Bill Amos. "The finest pacer I ever see!" continued the teamster. "An' if you don't beat that roan she-devil—now—" He choked.

"Look at her! By gosh, I didn't come all the way from Boston to see this colt get trimmed."

Bud looked at Chocorua. There she stood, ears back and head hung low, her eyes rolling wickedly at the grooms who toiled over her legs. She was fresh no longer.

Randall nodded at Bill in full agreement.

"Now look here, boy," said the veteran driver to Bud. "It would ruin some horses to give 'em the punishment that Cedar's takin' today. But I know him. Know his blood. Know his trainin'. He'll stand it. You beat the mare an' you've *won!*"

"Wh-what?" Bud gasped.

"Sure!" put in Amos. "It'll be decided on points. Take a look at that board, front o' the judges' stand."

Bud's eye followed his pointing finger, and a gust of hope swept through him. The board on the pavilion read:

	First Heat	Second Heat	Third Heat
SACO BOY	1	3	—
CHOCORUA	3	1	—
CEDAR	2	2	—

To put a figure "1" after Cedar's name in the third heat would give him a first and two seconds, while the best either of the others could make would be a first, a second, and a third.

With Long Bill helping him, Bud bent down and redoubled his efforts on the colt's legs. As he worked he whispered to the brave young horse, over and over, that

221

this time he *must*, and he felt Cedar's soft lips fumbling playfully at his ear.

The stand was in an uproar when the red colt and the roan mare went back for the final heat. But through the shouting Bud heard a deep, familiar bark and looked up to see the white terrier between Uncle John and Cal. The farmer was bent forward, his face gray and strained, and Cal was giving vent to shrill yells of encouragement. Bud waved a stiff mitten and went on as if in a dream.

Driven whirls of snow were cutting their faces as the jockeys turned above the start once more. Men along the track were huddled close together for warmth and thrashing their arms to shake off the numbness. It was blowing hard, and Bud knew the temperature must be near zero.

There were only two of them left to race, for Saco Boy had been withdrawn. Bud looked down the track through the white storm that hid the far-off grandstand and the town. The wind had swung to the northeast now, and into it they must go. The boy gathered the reins. Cedar's red haunches quivered into action. For the last time they crossed the starting-line.

How they got down to the half-mile post Bud never knew. The air was full of white, and snow particles bit at his eyelids, half blinding him. He was calling the colt's name again and again and leaning forward, always watching the roan mare's head where she raced alongside.

The smoothness was gone out of Cedar's gait. Every tired muscle of him was in revolt, and he was racked with

222

THE COLT'S GREAT HEART RESPONDED

a mighty effort at every stride. Yet on and on he held and never slackened. Into the final hundred yards they came at last, with the lean gray head still on their flank. And now the sorrel labored hard, his sides all streaked with frozen sweat, his head and neck stretched out. But he paced on with weary legs.

Cut by the whip, the mare came up desperately, inch by inch. Bud knew that no whip could better the valiant fight the red pacer was making. "Cedar—Cedar, boy!" he cried, and to the anguish of his voice some last reserve of the colt's great heart responded, for his nose was still beyond Chocorua's when they lunged under the line of the wire.

It was late afternoon of the day following Cedar's victory when Bud brought the colt home. Slant beams of frosty sunlight gleamed on a blanket of unbroken snow all up across the mountain's shoulder. The storm that had swept the speedway during the race had passed in the night.

Quietly, without effort, the good red pacer picked his way through the drifted snow of the hill road. Bud sat in the cutter and wondered if any boy had ever been quite as happy as he was at that moment. By his side was Tug, erect on the seat, looking businesslike and important. He had been elected to guard that thousand dollars, and he took his responsibility seriously.

There had been something of a ceremony when Bud

received the money. That was at the Road Horse Association Banquet in the evening. After seeing Cedar luxuriously rubbed and bedded down in the hotel stable Uncle John had returned to the farm with the Hunters. Bud, blushing and uncomfortable, had sat at the Governor's right hand throughout the dinner and listened to a great deal of horsy oratory, including many references to Cedar and himself. The great Congressman had shaken his hand and intoned something about "an honor to the old Granite State, both of you!" And then as a grand climax the toastmaster had placed Bud in the middle of a floral horseshoe and counted a score of crisp fifty-dollar bills into his hands.

All this had been gratifying enough to the boy's vanity, but the moment that meant most to him was still to come. They climbed the long hill and turned the last bend in the road, where the pasture pines grew close along the wall.

"Now, Cedar—now, boy—look your prettiest," breathed Bud as he gathered up the reins. And into the yard they swept, the colt all fire and grace, the boy grinning with pure ecstasy. Even Tug unbent enough to let out a joyful bark.

Uncle John pushed open the barn door and helped Bud unharness. Then together they went into the house. A moment later Bud was pouring handfuls of yellow bills into Aunt Sarah's lap. She beamed at him through misty glasses.

"I knew you'd do it," she said. "I knew you an' the colt had the spunk, between you," and she pulled his face down to kiss him.

"*Now*," cried Bud triumphantly—"*now* can I stay at Red Horse Hill for a while?"

Aunt Sarah chuckled, for it was an old joke of theirs.

"Just as long as you like," Uncle John replied. "Only remember," he added with a twinkle, "you're goin' to have a farm o' your own in a week or so."

"Gee, that's right!" said Bud. "Honest, I'd forgotten all about it. Did the papers come from Boston?"

"Everything came in yesterday, all in good order," the farmer replied. "An' I've been appointed your legal guardian. Now the only thing left is fer us to go over to Merriton tomorrow an' fix up those back taxes. The sheriff's sale was advertised fer day after tomorrow—the twenty-fifth. I'd like to see Sam Felton when he goes to buy in the property an' finds we've got there first!"

"So would I," laughed Bud, "especially after the trimming we gave his trotter. What train'll we take, Uncle John?"

The farmer considered. "I don't want you to miss any more school than you can help," he said at length. "If we caught the 1.10 to Merriton we'd be there a little after two. It shouldn't take more than an hour or so to git the whole thing fixed up. Then there's a four o'clock train comin' back, an' we'd be home by six, pretty close to chore time."

227

Bud went to bed early that evening, for between the banquet and the excitement of winning the race he had got very little sleep the night before. When he opened his window preparatory to climbing into bed he was surprised to see the stars obscured and snow-flakes gently falling outside.

"Ho hum!" he yawned. "Guess another inch or two won't hurt the sleighing." And he tumbled drowsily into his snug nest in the four-poster.

XXI

IT WAS still snowing at daybreak—not fast, but a steady, windless fall of white flakes. Six inches or more must have come in the night, and there was a still cold in the air. However, Bud was used to New Hampshire winters now. He dressed warmly, with a couple of hand-knitted sweaters under his mackinaw, pulled down his skating-cap over his ears, and started for school. "I'll meet you at the depot at one o'clock," he called back to Uncle John as he went out of the yard.

A blustery wind had begun to blow by the time Bud joined Cal at the Four Corners, and it seemed to increase in violence during their trip to Riverdale. Even above the talk and laughter of the youngsters in the barge, they could hear the angry howl of the gale. The last part of the journey was made slowly, for the horses were laboring through heavy drifts.

"Gee," said Bud as the boys went up the school steps, "this looks like a blizzard! I hope that train will be on time."

At noon he hurried through his lunch and explained

to the principal why he had to leave early. Then he started for the station. There was a lull in the storm and a few hardy householders and merchants were already out shoveling paths along the sidewalks. Bud was cheered at the sight of Uncle John's big black bearskin coat on the station platform.

The farmer's face wore a grave look as he turned to greet Bud. "I reckon we're both here in plenty o' time," he said. "They say all the trains are late. I drove down with the colt. He's over at Jones' Livery Stable. Well, it's cold out here; let's go inside."

They found a knot of men in the waiting-room, gathered about the ticket window.

"What's he say, Jud?" one of the group was asking the station agent. The telegraph instrument was clicking steadily, and the agent scribbled the message in pencil as it came in. When the clicking subsided he looked over the blank for a while, waving away eager questioners, then rose importantly and cleared his throat.

"Number Seven's stalled at Springvale," he announced. "Won't be through today. An' Number Nineteen won't make up until the plow gets through—prob'ly 'round nine o'clock tonight if it don't snow no more. Guess you fellers don't want them tickets after all, do you?"

A buzz of excited comment filled the dingy place. Uncle John's frown deepened. He drew Bud aside.

"I got a letter from Sheriff Gardner in this mornin's mail," he said. "He wanted us to be sure to git over to

Merriton today, because the sale had been advertised fer eleven o'clock tomorrow, an' there's no way he can call it off until you an' me have appeared personally to prove your title an' settle up those taxes. He says if it's a matter o' money he'll have the cash fer us. That's mighty good o' him, but o' course we don't need it now. What we do need is some way to git to Merriton before that sale."

He rubbed his hand over his chin thoughtfully. "If they git the tracks cleared so Number Nineteen can run we'll have to take that, even if it don't start till tonight. Let's see if we can hear any news around town."

They went out and plowed their way up the street to the Post Office. The usual crowd of men in fur coats and snowy arctics were gathered in the open floor before the rows of lock-boxes. The place was thick with smells— cigar smoke and wet coonskin predominating. Uncle John made his way through the group, greeting his friends as he went. As he neared the stamp window Jim Allen, the postmaster, caught sight of him and beckoned him and Bud back into the mail-sorting room. He was an old friend of Uncle John's.

"Look here," he said seriously, "what do you aim to do about that Hartley property, John?"

"Why," the farmer answered, "we're on our way to Merriton now to settle it. What made you ask?"

"Don't you know Sam Felton's goin' to try to bid it in?" said the postmaster.

"Yes," said Uncle John. "I understand he's got all the other bidders scared off. But we planned to git there ahead an' prove Bud's title to the farm. No trains are runnin', but Sam Felton's stuck here too, ain't he?"

Mr. Allen pursed his lips. "He's here now," he answered, "but I'm not so sure that he'll stay here."

"What do you mean, Jim?" the farmer asked.

"Well, if I was you, I'd have Bud run down to Hayes' Garage an' see if he notices anything special."

"Go ahead, Bud," Uncle John nodded.

The boy went out and ran down a side street leading to the town's principal auto repair shop. As he neared it he slackened his pace and tried to appear unconcerned. A number of loafers were standing about the cement floor, and in their midst Bud saw Felton's big yellow roadster. One rear wheel was jacked up and a mechanic was winding the huge tire with two-inch manila rope—a loop every six or eight inches. The other drive wheel had already been treated in like fashion. Dave Hayes was busy filling the tank behind the bucket seats with gasoline, and Gadway, Sam Felton's chauffeur, stood by, superintending operations.

Bud sauntered out again, turned the corner, and galloped back as fast as the drifts would permit. It was snowing once more and blowing as hard as ever.

In the back room of the Post Office the boy panted out his news.

Jim Allen nodded. "That's what I'd heard," he said.

232

"They say that thing can go through snow like a team of oxen only ten times as fast."

Uncle John looked at his watch, then turned to Bud decisively. "Here's a dollar to pay the stable," he said. "If Cedar's through with his dinner, hitch him up an' bring him here. Make sure he's been watered, too, an' put a half-bushel of oats in the sleigh. I'm goin' to telephone Hunter's and git 'em to take care of our stock tonight."

Fifteen minutes later Bud drove the big red colt up to the curb. "All right," Uncle John said as he swung into the sleigh, "we're startin' fer Merriton. Are you dressed warm enough?"

Bud assured him that he was. "How far is it by the road?" he asked.

"Thirty-two miles the shortest way," the farmer replied. "It'll be a long, cold ride, but we've got to do it."

Cedar was sober and businesslike. He seemed to sense the test ahead of him, for as they turned his head away from home he snorted once or twice, then settled down to an easy, rocking gait that soon had them clear of the town.

As they moved across the flat pine barrens toward the West Falls the wind blew fiercely, whipping sharp particles of snow against the sides of their faces. The outlines of the fences along the road seemed to shift in creeping eddies of white.

The way was new to Bud. It lay across a rolling plateau, a lonely place with a few farms scattered among

233

the pines. For the most part they followed a dim track between close-crowding woods. Save for the tinkle of their sleigh-bells and the soft, constant *hish-hs-sh* of the drifting snow the silence was unbroken.

They must have made six or seven miles when they heard a sound behind them. It was a low, throbbing roar that made the chill air vibrate.

"Whoa, boy," said Uncle John, and pulled the colt over to the side of the road so that they were partially screened by a birch thicket.

The noise grew louder, and looking back, Bud saw the car coming—a great yellow juggernaut plowing forward through the cloud of snow thrown from its whirling wheels.

Cedar shivered a little and the sleigh-bells rang, and though they could hardly have been heard above the thunder of the open exhaust, one of the figures in the low racing seats turned and looked at the sleigh. Then the man leaned forward suddenly and seemed to be speaking to the driver as the car pitched out of sight.

"Wasn't that Sam Felton?" asked Uncle John.

"Yes," said Bud. "I'd know that red fox-fur cap anywhere. He saw us, too."

Uncle John picked up the reins and Cedar settled into the harness once more. In a moment they were back on the road and jogging along in the deeply broken track of the automobile.

There was no abatement in the fury of the wind. If

anything it was blowing harder than ever—coming over in gusts of white that half blinded them while they were passing.

The farmer wisely gave the big colt his head and Cedar plowed forward without faltering. His strong red haunches moved as steadily as pistons. Bud was about to comment on how fresh the sorrel looked when suddenly the sleigh checked sharply and he saw Cedar floundering half out of sight in their first really big drift.

"There, boy, steady—steady," spoke Uncle John. The horse gathered himself and gave a great rearing plunge forward—once—twice—and he had pulled the cutter clear. He shook himself between the jingling shafts and went on.

The early dark was shutting down when they dipped into the Suncook Valley and came in sight of Depford Village. For hours they had seen no living thing in that world of white. Both Uncle John and Bud had settled into drowsy silence, half drugged by the cold and the steady forward motion of the sleigh. So it was that the next thing that happened came on them like a bad dream. Before they could rouse themselves to act it was over.

There was a sudden flurry in the snow close by Cedar's head, and with a tearing, snarling sound, a huge dark shape leaped for the horse's throat. Then came the vicious chop of teeth meeting on nothing. The big young stallion reared high on his hind legs, striking like lightning with both forefeet. There came another snarl that changed to

235

a hideous gasping yelp, and Cedar continued to plunge up and down with those sharp-shod pile-drivers of his.

Then in a moment it was all over. The red colt stood, shivering a little but quiet under Uncle John's soothing hand on the reins. Bud seized the whip with the loaded end up and waded ahead till he stood by Cedar's bridle. Deep in the snow before him was a misshapen thing that had once been a dog—a great, rangy brindled brute, cross-bred between collie and mastiff. Bud pulled the eighty-pound body out of the snow and heaved it to one side, and just as he did so he caught a glimpse of a man on snowshoes running uphill into the pines.

Uncle John had a dangerous glint in his eyes when he joined Bud. He had examined the horse and found that fortunately no damage had been done. After a minute he spoke.

"Any collar on that dog?" he asked.

"No," Bud said; "there was a place where one had been but it was gone." He told of the running figure he had seen, but the light had been too poor to make a clear description possible.

It had stopped snowing once more, and as they went down the long hill they could see the lights in huddled farmhouses twinkling between the roadside elms. Uncle John looked upward and sniffed the wind. "Still driftin'," he said, "an' overcast. In a few minutes it'll be black as Egypt's night. Nothin' fer it but to lay over here till daylight, I guess. We're 'most halfway."

236

Bud remembered that long yellow, leaping car ahead and the huge brass searchlight it carried, and his heart sank. Felton and Gadway would be able to push on even in the dark.

Uncle John turned in at a cozy-looking white house soon after they entered the town's main street. The place belonged to Mr. Schofield, a local merchant who had known the Masons for years. He was astonished to see them on such a night, but he quickly opened the stable door and helped them scrape the white crust of ice off Cedar's sides before they bedded his stall and gave him his oats.

Inside the warm lamp-lit house their story was soon told.

Mr. Schofield nodded when Uncle John mentioned Felton's car. "Yes," he said, "big yellow one, isn't it? Went past here an hour or so ago, and when I came home from the store I saw it in the blacksmith shop down by the railroad. Looked like they were havin' trouble, too, for some one was under the car, hammerin' at the insides. Maybe Friend Sam won't get to Merriton tonight after all."

It was a little later, as they sat at the supper table, that Uncle John turned to their host with a question. "Anybody here in the village own a big, mean, brindle dog?" he asked.

Mr. Schofield considered. "Let's see," he said, "brindle —mm—white patch on his chest? Cropped ears?"

237

"Yes," Bud put in eagerly, "that's the dog."

"Well," he replied, "if you saw *him* I hope he was chained. Worst brute I ever set eyes on. Old Ahab Rowe owns him, up above the village a mile or so. The dog went ugly a year ago and mighty nigh killed a horse that was drivin' by. Since then he's been kept in old man Rowe's back yard with a big trace-chain on his collar.

"Ahab is kind o' cracked himself. He's got a no-account timber lot he's tryin' to sell. I understand one o' the big lumber companies has been dickerin' with him. By George, come to think of it, 'twas Felton's company!"

"All right," Uncle John interrupted; "I think I can guess the rest. They knew he'd do anything they told him to sell the lot, an' when they come roarin' through in their chariot o' fire all they had to do was tip him the word. They figgered correct that the dog would be let loose on us. Only"—he smiled grimly—"only they forgot to reckon with Cedar.

"An' so," he concluded after a pause, "we left that brindle dog back there in the snow a ways. He'd been stepped on some."

After a walk down the street that evening Mr. Schofield reported that the mighty racing-car was still undergoing repairs, while Gadway and Felton walked up and down and swore at the blacksmith. There was nothing more for Uncle John and Bud to do; so they said good night about nine o'clock and went to bed.

In no time at all, as it seemed to Bud, he was shaken

238

awake. It was still night, but a faint radiance was in the room. "It's cleared, an' the moon's up," said Uncle John. "Better hustle into your clothes."

As the boy dressed in the frosty atmosphere of the bedroom he stole a glance at his watch. It was just four o'clock.

Mr. Schofield was also up, and by the time Cedar had been harnessed there was some coffee for them in the kitchen. The village lay silent under the moon as they went out of the yard.

From Depford to Merriton, Uncle John told Bud, it was twenty miles by the valley road. But by taking a short way over the hills it was possible to cut the distance to sixteen miles, and it was this route that he proposed to follow. He took the right-hand fork when they reached Hansonville, and they crossed the river through the covered bridge.

Up the long hills beyond lay the snow, crested here and there with drifts, unbroken by any track. The wind had died down. They could hear Cedar's breathing, deep and quick, as he strove forward and up—always up, it seemed now. Bud had a pair of snowshoes, borrowed from Mr. Schofield, and now he put them on and broke the trail for the horse where the going was worst.

At the top of the ridge they stopped to rest. They had been a good two hours making the first seven miles, and now the roosters were crowing below them in the valley.

239

A faint light began to dim the brightness of the stars. Bud was undoing the last snowshoe thong when Uncle John held up his hand in a quick gesture. "Hark!" he whispered. Bud rose, listening tensely. An intermittent rumble like the muttering of a thunder-storm a long way off came to his ears, and he knew it was the sound of the great yellow roadster roaring down the valley.

"Blacksmith must have worked all night," said Uncle John tersely. "I reckon they'll stick to the Suncook road; so we aren't likely to see 'em again."

But he was wrong. In the next five minutes they heard that noise often, and each time it drifted to their ears it sounded louder, more menacing. The road was winding through a rough country of birch and pine. There were frequent narrow places and treacherous gullies.

Of a sudden the terrific bellow of Felton's exhaust broke out right behind them. He had taken the hill road, following their track. Bud looked back quickly. The roadster was coming fast despite the snow, throwing a great spray of white to either side. They were in a comparatively smooth bit of road, and Uncle John pulled over to the right to allow plenty of room. He had the whip in his left hand. Then as Bud watched, the huge V-shaped radiator, like the prow of a destroyer, veered in their direction.

"Look out!" he yelled.

Uncle John brought down the whip and Cedar jumped —forward and sidewise like a cat. They were tipped out

240

of the sleigh, unhurt, but the wheels fairly brushed them as the car plowed by.

"Thought they might try that," said Uncle John. His mouth was set in a hard line as they righted the cutter and started on.

For half a mile they could hear the diminishing rumble of the motor. Then suddenly it ceased. When they came to the top of another hill and looked down the far side they understood the reason. The road wound down through a narrow ravine, the steep sides of which were dotted with sparse hardwood growth. And halfway down the hill, at a place where the banks were a bare five yards apart, the great car wallowed, helpless. Its nose was almost touching the trunk of a fallen maple, lodged squarely across the road.

They drove slowly down the hill till they were some fifty yards above the prostrate tree. There they got out, and Uncle John led Cedar across a stone wall and up the steep bank. The big colt made it in one splendid fiery dash. Picking their way between the trees, they brought the sleigh to a stop just opposite the stranded car.

Below, in the road, Felton and Gadway were scurrying here and there in an aimless fashion, pausing only for the delivery of such swear words as occurred to them. Gadway chopped futilely at the two-foot rock maple trunk with a stillson wrench. The lumber magnate meanwhile gathered a little pile of sticks and bark under the tree and tried to light a fire with safety matches.

241

Uncle John watched for a while, and his grim look gave place to one of mild interest. At length he spoke.

"Sam," he called, "if you'd played fair, I'd be tempted to give you a ride as far as the courthouse in Merriton. But things bein' as they are I guess I'll just let you an' your friend camp out here fer a spell. If you ever git that fire goin' the tree'll burn well. Ought to last till about tomorrow afternoon. Well, Sam, I've got business to attend to. See you later. If you're willin' to make a fair price, maybe the boy'll agree to sell you the timber on that Hartley place sometime."

They descended into the road beyond the fallen log. There Uncle John clucked tranquilly to the red colt, and they set out once more for Merriton. Two hours later, as he rocked along up the bustling street of the countyseat, Cedar snorted proudly and tossed his gallant head. A tall figure on the pavement turned and hailed them. It was the sheriff.

"Well, John!" he cried. "How long you been in town? I was gittin' worried. You must've driven over before the big storm. The colt seems to like to git out an' warm up, don't he?"

"Yep," chuckled Uncle John, "he sure does enjoy his little mornin' constitutional!"

.   .   .   .

It is always hard to finish a story, but here this one must end.

How Bud grew up on Red Horse Hill, how the sale

242

of the white pine timber from his farm put him through college and helped to make the Mason and Martin dairy herd famous over half of New England, how Cedar raced for two glorious seasons on the Grand Circuit and broke the two-minute mark to win at Syracuse—these are other stories in themselves.

Cedar is an old horse now. His nose is gray, and he

spends long summer days drowsing in the green paddock behind the great white barns. But when winter comes and the bells jingle over the packed snow of the speed-way Bud still harnesses the good red horse and lets him pace. With him now in the cutter he takes his own boys. And a big white terrier, grandson of brave old Tug, runs alongside as they go down the snow path.

Cedar moves a bit stiffly at first. But as his ancient legs

warm to their work there is a hint of past battles won in the vigor of his rocking stride. Old-timers turn to watch him with a mistiness in their eyes. And though their lips are silent, their hearts are lifted in a toast: "The road-horse—may he never die!"